When nurse Joanna Merivale went to Ireland to nurse Roger Carnehill, it was at first just another job to her. But in that job her first thought was to give of her best— something that looked impossible in the household full of emotional problems in which she found herself. There was her patient, cruelly frustrated by his accident; Magda, mocking and sophisticated; and René, generous and unselfish. And to add to all these difficulties, Joanna soon found that her own emotions were to be involved as deeply as everyone else's . . .

D1111902

BY YET ANOTHER DOOR

Jane Arbor

ATLANTIC LARGE PRINT
Chivers Press, Bath, England.
Curley Publishing, Inc.,
South Yarmouth, Mass., USA.

Library of Congress Cataloging-in-Publication Data

Arbor, Jane.
  By yet another door / Jane Arbor.
    p.   cm.—(Atlantic large print)
  ISBN 0–7927–0608–0 (lg. print)
  1. Large type books.   I. Title.
[PR6051.R25B9   1991]
823′.914—dc20

                                                          90–27322
                                                          CIP

British Library Cataloguing in Publication Data available

This Large Print edition is published by Chivers Press, England, and
Curley Publishing, Inc, U.S.A. 1991

Published by arrangement with Harlequin Enterprises B.V.

U.K. Hardback ISBN 0 7451 8109 0
U.K. Softback ISBN 0 7451 8121 X
U.S.A. Softback ISBN 0 7927 0608 0

CHAPTER ONE

Off the ten-twenty-eight from Dublin that morning there was only one passenger for Tulleen—a girl, who on finding the platform and station yard empty, set down her suitcase in annoyance.

She had been travelling since yesterday afternoon, arriving in Dublin in a bleak, unwelcoming dawn, had breakfasted five hours ago and *surely*, when she had given the precise time of her arrival at Tulleen, the Carnehills might have made some arrangements for meeting her?

With the politeness which showed he had no more urgent call upon his attention than to help her the stationmaster asked:

'Now it's something that you'd be wanting, miss?'

'Yes, a taxi, please. For Carrieghmere. I'm supposed to be there in time for lunch.'

His old eyes were turned upon her in benevolent curiosity. 'Carrieghmere? Now you'd be a visitor, like?'

'I'm going as nurse to Mr. Roger Carnehill.' Joanna's tone was clipped and businesslike. 'How far is it to Carrieghmere?'

But her question was ignored by the stationmaster.

'Ah, Master Roger, is it? There's the sad

1

thing, now! That such a fine young man in the joy of his youth should have come by such a terrible accident that laid him on his back these many months! To think that our eyes may never again be gladdened by the sight of him, riding through Tulleen with the pride of the wind in his hair—!'

Joanna cut in crisply: 'I hadn't understood that Mr. Carnehill was a permanent invalid. I expect to find him nearly convalescent when I get to Carrieghmere. But now—how do I get there? Could I walk?' she asked.

'Arrah, you couldn't walk. 'Tis all of seven miles, but it's Wednesday, and McKiley'll be out from Carrieghmere any minute now to put the eggs on the one o'clock train. There now, you can go back with him. Maybe Mrs. Carnehill meant it to be that way all the while!'

'Maybe,' commented Joanna dryly, thinking, all the same, that it was an odd and casual arrangement to be expected of people as wealthy as she believed the Carnehills to be. Meanwhile, who was Mr. McKiley?

He was the agent for the Carrieghmere estate, her informant told her. She had only to wait...

Reflecting that she had already done quite a lot of this already, Joanna refused an invitation to go in and sit by the ticket-office fire. 'I'll look out for Mr. McKiley here,' she said, and wandered out into the rain, wanting to stretch her legs after the long journey.

So this was Ireland! And so far, true to all the traditional pictures of it. Casual, easy-going and, if the immediate surroundings of Tulleen station were anything to go by, revelling in a comfortable squalor which seemed to worry nobody.

Carrieghmere would be different, of course. For Carrieghmere was an estate commanding an acreage which would spell imposing wealth in England. And old Colonel Kimstone, who had been exclusively her patient in the London nursing home from which Matron had sent her to this post, had spoken glowingly to Matron of the comfort she would know there.

She went on down the street, looking about her and becoming aware of a curious scent in her nostrils. Rather pleasant! She sniffed at it experimentally and then realized that it was the smell of peat smoke and that, with it, Ireland—the strange country—was indeed about her.

At the sound of a car in the distance she began to retrace her steps. But when a luxurious saloon of American make swept past her, she decided that it would not contain the expected Mr. McKiley, who was only the agent for Carrieghmere and would probably deliver farm produce in a shooting brake or a van. However, when she reached the station yard, there stood the Lincoln, while a man in riding-breeches and tweed coat unloaded egg-cases.

She stood near by, watching him until he sensed her presence and looked up.

'Good morning,' said Joanna with a smile.

'Good morning.' He took his hat from his head, and there was a flash of very white teeth beneath a clipped black moustache. His eyes passed over her in a single inquiring glance.

She explained: 'If you are Mr. McKiley I think I'm going to have to ask you to take me back to Carrieghmere. My name is Merivale—Nurse Merivale, and I dare say you'll have heard that I'm expected.'

Again the swift glance swept over her, and again the smile flashed out. Then he held out a hand.

'Yes, I'm Justin McKiley. I suppose old Thomasoy told you I'd be along. And I'd certainly heard that a nurse was expected, though forgive me!'—he sketched a bow towards her—'I hadn't looked to see anyone quite like you.'

Joanna ignored the implied compliment to ask briskly:

'Well, could we go soon, please? I'm supposed to arrive in time for lunch.'

He gave her an odd look and then said casually: 'Time enough. Thomasoy can see these things on to the train and then we'll be off. You won't get your lunch until near three, anyway. At The House they usually eat

4

when it's ready, or when they feel like it—not before. So don't worry yourself. You won't be late. Unless, of course, you'd care to have lunch with me?'

Joanna shook her head. 'Thank you, no. I should have been there before this. My train came in at twelve.'

For a moment his conventionally handsome face looked almost sulky. Then he shrugged. 'All right, have it your own way. Only don't suppose that anyone will have flattened themselves with anxiety, waiting for you. Get into the car now, and I'll be back in two shakes.'

Joanna fetched her suitcase and set it near the open trunk before slipping into the seat beside the driver's. She leaned back, feeling suddenly very tired and extremely hungry. She gave a rueful little sigh. She had often been out to cases before, but this was surely her oddest reception yet! She would certainly have something to write to Dale about when she got to the end of this day!

'Well now,' said her companion as he accelerated and tore down the village street at a pace which scattered children and hens impartially, 'let's be hearing about you. You came off the twelve-four and you're bound for the job of nursing Roger? How are you going to like that?'

'I usually enjoy my cases,' she said non-committally.

5

He glanced at her mockingly. 'That was a very professional touch. It said. "Get to your corner, Justin McKiley!" All right. You haven't met Roger? No, you couldn't have, of course. What about Mrs. Carnehill? Do you know her?'

'No. I nursed a Colonel Kimstone, who I believe is a neighbour of Mrs. Carnehill's, when he was in the Marrone Nursing Home in London. It was he who recommended me to her as a nurse to Mr. Carnehill.'

'M'm. Old Kimstone lives twenty miles away across the bog. But—as you'll find—that does constitute near neighbourhood around here.' He nodded out of the car window on his own side. 'That's part of the bog there. And if you look out on your side and crane your neck you'll see the Wicklows in the distance. Or maybe you won't, in the rain.'

But Joanna did as she was told and believed that, despite the driving mist, she could distinguish the blue line of the hills on the horizon.

'Of course you'll have seen them from the sea, coming over,' he suggested.

'No. It was still dark when we got in.'

He turned and looked at her. 'You'll be tired, so. What about stopping in for lunch with me? Mine will at least be ready!'

But Joanna was firm. 'No, I mustn't do that.' She added politely: 'I think the

6

stationmaster said you were Mr. Carnehill's agent? Do you live on the estate?'

'Yes. In the Dower House. I'll show it to you as we go past.' As Justin McKiley spoke, he turned in at an open gateway between tall stone pillars.

'That's it,' he said. But Joanna had only the briefest glance towards a small house among the trees to her right when the avenue broadened into a sweep of rather weedy gravel before a grey stone house of imposing size.

'Carrieghmere!' he announced as he took out her suitcase and led the way up the wide shallow steps and into a big hall, the atmosphere of which struck coldly to Joanna's travel-tiredness.

Nobody came out to meet them, so Justin McKiley went across to a fine carved door upon the right, flung it open and called to someone within:

'I picked up Miss Merivale at Tulleen. She's been travelling all night and she says she was expected to lunch. I'll leave her with you now, may I?'

Through the open door Joanna could see a woman, who had been kneeling on the hearth before a brightly glowing fire, suddenly spring to her feet with an exclamation.

'There!' she said. 'And I wrote it down—"Meet the twelve-four Wednesday." Wait now—I have it here!' From a mass of

7

papers on the desk behind her she drew out a minute scrap of paper and handed it to McKiley.

He looked at it and gave it back to her. 'It says Thursday,' he remarked dryly.

'*No*? So it does, at that. And the poor girl arriving and not met at all! Let me get at her. You say you brought her up, Justin?'

Without waiting for a reply she pushed past him and came out to where Joanna stood.

She was a short plump woman with a bright colour and deep-set blue eyes below the curling grey fringe of hair on her forehead. She wore a checked apron over a green dress that was unnecessarily fussy, and about her throat she wore a string of pearls which Joanna guessed were real.

'There now, what a welcome! And Roger looking forward to your coming for days! It's all my fault.' The blue eyes twinkled. 'But it usually is, isn't it, Justin?'

The man looked a trifle bored. 'If you say so,' he remarked, adding meaningly: 'Miss Merivale still hasn't had her lunch, you know.'

'Weren't you telling me that, first thing?' she rebuked. 'She'll get it now, as soon as I have it ready. You off, Justin? When will you be in to see Roger again? Come to dinner tomorrow night? Then you can meet Miss Merivale properly.'

'What time?' he asked laconically.

8

'Oh—about half-past seven.'

'I don't mean what time shall I come. I mean, what time am I likely to get my dinner?'

Joanna reflected that if the woman in the checked apron and the pearls were indeed Mrs. Carnehill, as she supposed must be the case, she was extraordinarily tolerant of her agent's casual, offhand manner. But she seemed quite unmoved.

'Be off with you now,' she said briskly. 'Come at eight if that seems safer to you. Miss Merivale—or would you rather be called Nurse?—you come along with me.'

Joanna followed her into the room from which she had come. To the girl's surprise, her employer went over to the hearth and picked up a closed grilling grid, upon the bars of which reposed a luscious-looking steak.

'There!' she said with pride. 'That'll be your lunch. I cook it in here instead of letting them do it in the kitchen, because the fire gets brighter, and I'm old-fashioned enough to like to grill on top instead of underneath.'

She went on conversationally: 'You'll want to see Roger, of course. But you shan't go until you've had something to eat and a rest. He rests too after lunch, anyway.'

'How does Mr. Carnehill seem?' asked Joanna.

The bright eyes clouded. 'I—don't know. You'll see for yourself, Nurse. Dr. Beltane

9

tries to be encouraging, and his surgeon from Dublin comes out occasionally, too. We've got him downstairs, of course, ready for when he uses the wheelchair—'

'Oh, doesn't he get about yet?' Joanna's surprise sounded in her voice. 'I thought Matron understood that he was convalescent, that the case would only be a matter of a week or two?'

'You mean *you've* come only for a week or two?' Mrs. Carnehill looked at her in dismay.

'Why, no. I—Well, of course I shall stay as long as Mr. Carnehill needs nursing.'

Mrs. Carnehill looked relieved at her reply. 'That's all right then, but I'm afraid you will be here for longer than a week or two, so I hope you'll be happy with us. There now! The steak is just about done. I'll call someone to show you to your room and we'll meet in the dining-room.' She bustled out and came back bringing a fat Irishwoman with her.

'This is Cook,' she announced. 'Roseen—the housemaid—has a day off, so Cook will show you to your room before she helps me to dish up.'

Cook clutched the handle of Joanna's suitcase in a brawny fist. 'This way, will ye?' she demanded, and marched ahead of Joanna up the broad oak staircase.

It was with pleased surprise that the girl saw the bedroom which had been allotted to her. It was not too large, the two broad

10

windows would face south, she thought, and there was a pleasant pale green carpet on the floor, a colouring which was taken up by the curtains and the cushions in an easy chair by the fireplace. About it there was none of the rather austere chill of such of the ground floor as she had seen.

Downstairs, in the dining-room, she was to be surprised again. The room itself was big, not too warm and its furnishings were heavy and near-Victorian. But the appointments of the table—the silver, the glass, the linen—were exquisite. The steak which had been cooked in such an unorthodox fashion lay in a silver chafing-dish, and the sight told Joanna's young, healthy appetite that waiting for it had been worth it.

Mrs. Carnehill intercepted her glance at the big clock on the mantelshelf.

'You'll get used to this,' she said comfortably. 'Over here we frequently don't lunch till half-past two or three.' She went on: 'Shuan isn't here today. She has gone to Naas market to sell some of her rabbits and bring back the horsemeat for the dogs. So I couldn't *really* have met you myself off the train today, because she has got the car. It was indeed fortunate that it happened to be Wednesday and that Justin—'

Her voice trailed off vaguely and Joanna ventured to ask:

'Who is Shuan?'

'Shuan? Oh, she's my ward. Her parents died when she was twelve, and she has lived with us ever since. She's seventeen—no, eighteen—now. She makes her own pocket-money with her rabbits and her dog-breeding, and sometimes she has given riding lessons to visitors to Tulleen, if they want them. She helps me too. Between us, we've managed all the winter, but I have to be away a lot—to Dublin and sometimes over to England—and I couldn't leave her entirely responsible for Roger. So that's why we needed you.'

'You have to go to England on business?' asked Joanna politely.

Her hostess looked a little surprised. 'Oh—didn't Colonel Kimstone tell you about me?'

'No, I don't think so,' smiled Joanna.

Mrs. Carnehill threw back her head and laughed. 'Then *how* you must have wondered whether I was to be trusted with the steak!' she gurgled. 'Why, I'm "Luculla"! My *job* is food. You *must* have heard of me!'

Joanna had. She had had her mouth made to water by articles on cookery, signed 'Luculla,' in innumerable magazines in England. She told her companion so, and looked at her with fresh interest, though at the back of her mind hovered the question which had been troubling her for some time. Where *was* the wealth and luxury which she

12

had expected to find at Carrieghmere? A household which apparently commanded the use of only one car, a hostess who was a journalist and whose ward gave riding lessons in order to make money—nothing of all this seemed to tie up with the valuable and antique appointments of the lunch table, nor with those pearls about her employer's throat, nor indeed with the fact of an agent who could afford to possess and use an expensive American car.

Joanna knew that none of this was any business of hers, but though she tried to dismiss it from her mind it made her all the more curious to meet the member of the household who was to be her special care—Roger Carnehill. She was glad, therefore, when at the end of the meal his mother said:

'Now you would like to see Roger, I dare say?'

'Yes, I should.' Joanna hesitated. 'Would you like me to get into uniform first?'

Mrs. Carnehill looked vague. 'I don't think so. You look charming as you are. And I want Roger to like you—not to feel that he's being regimented. I think maybe that you'll see why, when you've known him for a little while.'

She led the way to another room on the ground floor, of which, Joanna's swift professional glance told her, the furnishings were far too heavy for a sick room and that it was woefully overcrowded.

The overcrowding was due partly to the presence of three large dogs, one of which, an Irish setter, lumbered off the foot of the bed as they entered.

'Dogs! Dogs!' protested Mrs. Carnehill half-heartedly as they surrounded Joanna and flung their forepaws almost to her shoulder. 'Roger, call them off. Miss Merivale may not like dogs.'

The young man in the bed lowered the book he had been reading.

'Then maybe they won't like her,' he said in a deep, attractive voice. 'What then?'

'But I do,' said Joanna with a smile. She looked at her new patient with interest. And he looked at her.

For some reason she had misread her instructions about him. She had expected him to be a mere boy—not much over twenty, if that. But he looked nearer thirty—a man with a thin face, a stubbornly formed jawline and a petulant mouth. His eyes were as blue as his mother's, but his hair was red—a mass of flaming 'carrots'. He ran his hand rather wearily through it as he looked at Joanna.

With her smile Joanna said: 'How do you do?' and he returned a 'How do you do' of his own. Then he turned to his mother. 'You said Miss Merivale wasn't coming till tomorrow,' he accused.

14

'I know. I got muddled. But Justin was over to Tulleen with the eggs, and he brought her back.'

'Oh, he did? Did he say when he was coming in to see me?'

'I asked him to dinner tomorrow night—to meet Miss Merivale.'

Roger Carnehill raised his eyebrows. 'I thought he'd met her,' he commented ironically. 'Anyway, send him in to see me afterwards, will you? Where's Shuan?'

'At Naas, darling. It's market-day, you know.'

Joanna stood silently by, using her trained observation to the full. In the sharply put questions she thought she detected the typical invalid's effort to reach out beyond his bed, to keep a finger, as it were, upon the pulse of events over which he no longer had control.

She realized that she knew less than she ought about the course of his illness. She would have to ask when she could see their Doctor Beltane, in order to get instructions. She knew only that a riding accident of nearly two years earlier had resulted in spinal trouble from which he ought by now to have recovered, but apparently hadn't, even to the extent of convalescence. It looked, certainly, as if her own work towards his recovery might be of indefinite duration. Momentarily she believed she would not mind—even if it meant that she would be away from

15

London—and from Dale—for far longer than she had expected.

Mrs. Carnehill was saying: 'Fancy! She didn't know about my being Luculla!' She sounded as amused as she had been at lunch, but Roger frowned slightly as he said to Joanna:

'Didn't you? Hadn't Colonel Kimstone told you?'

'No. I haven't seen the Colonel since I nursed him, and that was some time ago. He didn't mention Carrieghmere then,' she told him.

'Then you didn't know that Mother spends her time poking about the markets in the back streets of Dublin and writing about food for people who probably don't know the difference between a consommé and a pig's trotter?' His words might have been humorous if it were not for the bitter, sarcastic ring in his voice.

Joanna was shocked. It was clear that there was some conflict between mother and son on the subject, and Joanna was anxious not to be drawn into 'taking sides'. But she had begun to admire Mrs. Carnehill tremendously and she resented her son's criticism.

'It's the people like that who most need to be told what the difference is—' she began with conviction, but her patient broke in with a sarcastic:

'And I suppose they have to look to a

16

Carnehill of Carrieghmere to tell them!'

'If a Carnehill of Carrieghmere is willing and knowledgeable enough to tell them—why not?' retorted Joanna.

He looked at her, not replying, and Mrs. Carnhill put in briskly:

'Come now, Roger. We've been over all this so often before. And I still say I like food; I like discovering odd ways of cooking it and, best of all, I like passing on my tips to other people—'

She stopped, but not before Joanna had noticed the tightening of the sick man's grip upon the coverlet. He said irritably:

'But it's all so absurd. It was all right when it was merely a hobby with you, but surely there should be plenty for you to attend to here, now that I'm no use? I ought to be able to look to you to be my link with what's going on on the estate. But as it is, there seems to be a conspiracy lately to keep things back from me. I even have to *force* a report out of my own agent!'

'Roger—*please*!' For the first time Mrs. Carnehill seemed distressed. 'You know it isn't like that at all. It's simply that neither Justin nor I see the necessity for bothering you with trifles—'

'Nor with anything else, it seems,' he returned gloomily, and Joanna felt that it was time she intervened. She turned to Mrs. Carnehill, saying quietly:

17

'Oughtn't Mr. Carnehill to rest now? Then, when I've changed into my uniform, perhaps you would show me where I prepare his tea.'

'Yes, of course. We'll go now, Roger. Try to sleep a little, won't you?' Mrs. Carnehill moved to the head of the bed and laid a hand lightly upon his shoulder. He did not speak, but he looked up at her, and Joanna guessed that some unspoken word of communion had passed between them.

More and more she was coming to admire the unexpected dignity of the older woman, so that she was completely unprepared for the sudden crumpling of her bright features as the sickroom door closed behind them.

She leaned back against the oak and whispered with a kind of desperate tiredness:

'It's my fault. I've never learnt that any discussion of my work irritates him beyond measure. And this morning began well enough. It'll be my fault entirely if by nightfall he has one of his black moods upon him—' She looked up at Joanna, a wry smile at her lips. 'I told you that Roger wouldn't be regimented. You'll find that he won't even accept the limitations of his illness; he'll still indulge in the most absurd indignations and self-pity, not seeing at all that they only hold him back!'

'It's *because* he's ill that he can work himself into passions like that,' Joanna told her gently. 'And he's been ill for a very long time!'

'But really he has had every care—mine, Shuan's—everything we could do for him!'

'And now he's got me!' commented Joanna dryly.

The older woman looked at her, her face composed again. 'Yes. Now he has you.' She hesitated. Then: 'D'you know, I'm still not sure what I ought to call you? Nurse? Miss Merivale? What would you like?'

Then Joanna did something which was against all the strict canons of nursing etiquette at the Marrone Nursing Home, and which would have struck horror in Matron's professional breast.

She said: 'Call me Joanna, won't you?'

CHAPTER TWO

When Joanna took in his tea later on Roger Carnehill made no reference to his earlier outburst.

His eyes ran over her uniform as he said provocatively: 'I suppose, now I'm taken over officially, so to speak, I become the patient in bed number so-and-so? Meanwhile, what am I to call you, when I don't say "you"? What does Mother call you?'

'I asked her to call me Joanna.'

'Joanna?' He repeated the name slowly as if

weighing its quality. Then: 'Why shouldn't I do the same? Wouldn't it make for mateyness all round?'

For an instant her blue eyes met his grey ones. She said briskly:

'If it made for co-operation, it would be quite a good idea. If it didn't—'

'If it didn't, it would merely be familiar of me! Is that it—*Joanna*?'

Joanna had to laugh as she handed him his tea-cup. 'Call me what you like—or whatever comes first to your mind,' she said easily. 'Meanwhile, won't you tell me about your day? What time you usually wake, what your routine has been?'

He raised his eyebrows. 'Oh—d'you mean you're not going to reorganize it according to some starchy cut-and-dried methods of your own?'

'I can't promise,' returned Joanna placidly. 'But begin at the beginning—what time *do* you wake?'

'Oh—about seven, I suppose. If I've been sleeping, that is. If I haven't, and Shuan comes too early with the tea, she knows she'll get slung out on her ear, because I may have just dropped off.'

'So Shuan—I'm afraid I don't know her other name—brings your morning tea?'

'Ferrall. Shuan Ferrall,' he prompted laconically. 'She hauls the dogs in, and some extra saucers, and we all sit round having a

20

cosy conversazione.'

'The dogs? All of them?' queried Joanna.

'Not,' returned her patient gravely, 'not all seventeen. Only these three. They always come.'

'I see,' said Joanna just as gravely. 'And after that, I suppose they spend their day here? Or do they ever feel the need to step outside for a breath of air?'

He laughed. 'All right, you win that round! You don't approve of their being here, do you? I saw you look down your nose at them when you came in with Mother. Well, you'll have to fight Shuan about that. They're her animals; she believes I adore having 'em around, and I wouldn't disillusion her for the world—'

He broke off as swift footsteps sounded in the hall outside, and the door opened with a clatter of its handle. Joanna looked up to see a girl—Shuan Ferrall, no doubt—standing upon the threshold.

She wore jodhpurs, a clumsily darned fawn jumper and a short jacket shrugged across her shoulders. She was hatless, and her black hair, dishevelled by the wind, made a tangle of curls in her neck. Her cheeks were flushed to a high colour, and Joanna, looking at her, realized that greenish-blue eyes deeply set beneath dark curling lashes could indeed appear to have been 'smudged in' by a careless hand.

21

For a second Shuan stood there. Then in one convulsive movement she flung herself across the room, bent over Roger Carnehill and kissed him upon the lips.

'*Darling*!' she exclaimed. 'What *do* you think—?'

Unceremoniously he set the tips of his fingers at the roots of her hair where it sprang upward from her brow, and held her back from him.

'I don't,' he said. 'Your volatility would disturb anybody's thought-processes. If it's affectation or nerves, or both—check it. It grows on you. Speak nicely to Miss Merivale now.'

She flicked him lightly upon the cheek.

'Beast,' she commented briefly.

Her violent embrace of Roger had dislodged her jacket. It had fallen at the feet of Joanna, who now handed it to her with a smile.

She smiled back a little uncertainly.

'Oh, you're Roger's nurse!' she said. 'I ought to have known, but I didn't expect you until tomorrow. None of us did, did we, Roger?' As she turned to appeal to him her eyes lighted upon the tea-tray.

'Why, you've got tea!' she accused. 'Whatever for? Didn't you eat your lunch?' She looked curiously from him to Joanna and back again, and Roger said with a glance of his own towards Joanna:

22

'Apparently it's an old English custom. Over there, four o'clock tea is something of a rite, I understand!'

'But it isn't four o'clock! It's nearer six!'

'That,' Roger pointed out—and Joanna had an uncomfortable feeling that he was talking 'at' her, rather that 'to' Shuan—'is not the fault of our charming new English broom! We didn't lunch until two-forty-five or so.'

'Well, I didn't lunch at all. I went shopping and spent more than I meant to, on a powder-bowl I wanted to give to Mums. That's what I call Mrs. Carnehill,' she explained with rapid politeness to Joanna. 'So I didn't really have enough money left for lunch; I bought some chocolate and ate it on the way home. But I'm still starving. Pass me a biscuit, Roger—there's a dear!'

She munched greedily and then said again: 'What do you think? Wait now, till I tell you. I've sold the whole of Bambina's next litter—when it arrives.'

'Who to?' asked Roger ungrammatically.

'That woman breeder from Athlone who bought the others. She was in Naas today, and I met her.' She stirred one of the dogs on the floor gently with her foot.

'Be an angel, Bambina, and produce a lot!' she urged.

Again Roger Carnehill glanced obliquely at Joanna, a look which she caught, but which for the moment she did not understand. It

23

was with a kind of impish provocation that he said meaningly:

'Maybe Bambina will, maybe she won't. The even tenor of her way is likely to be upset. At any minute now she may be dismissed from the presence!'

Shuan had knelt in order to caress the dog's silky golden ears. But at his words she looked up sharply. 'Dismissed? What do you mean? What has she done?'

He shrugged his shoulders and threw another significant glance in Joanna's direction. '*I'm* not dismissing her,' he said.

The girl's look of inquiry shifted too, while a dark flush rose slowly from her throat to her face.

'But Bambina is always allowed in here,' she protested. 'So are the other two. Have *you* said they're not to come any more?'

For a moment or two Joanna did not reply. She felt puzzled, and she was annoyed with her patient for having twisted this barb of irritation from something she had not said. As equably as she could, she said:

'*I've* given no orders about the dogs.'

'But you've wanted to! Your first impression was—quite obviously—"Too much furniture. Too much dog." Wasn't it, now?' challenged Roger.

Aware that her first thoughts had indeed been along such lines, Joanna still managed to say evenly: 'I didn't realize that I was so

24

transparent, and first impressions aren't always to be relied upon, are they? In any case, I haven't any authority to give orders, except under Dr. Beltane's instructions.'

Shuan was looking from one to the other bewilderedly.

'Well, Beltie knows all about the dogs,' she put in defiantly. 'They've always been here when he's come to see Roger. Surely you don't mean to put it into his mind now that they oughtn't to come in—that they're unhealthy or anything!'

Calmly Joanna held out her hand for Roger's cup, set it on the tray which she picked up. As she turned towards the door she smiled at Shuan, deliberately leaving Roger out.

'Do believe that I've said nothing at all about the dogs being here or not,' she said in a conciliatory tone. 'Mr. Carnehill knows that quite well. I daresay he's only teasing.'

But there was no answering smile from the girl. She looked hurt and apprehensive—far more so than the little misunderstanding warranted. It was as if she had suddenly seen Joanna as an intruder, as a threat to some way of life or habit which she treasured. At a gesture from Roger she moved over to open the door for Joanna, but she said nothing at all.

Outside, Joanna was surprised to find that her hands holding the tray were trembling

25

very slightly. She disliked scenes and was inclined to blame herself completely for any which involved a patient. But *had* the one which had just passed been in any way her fault? Surely not. It had been Roger Carnehill who had used his too-keen perception to bait her. He had deliberately created that 'brush' of hostility between her and the younger girl!

She began to think about Roger Carnehill, being caught into the interest of him as a case, and being anxious, out of her newly awakened liking and admiration for his mother, to do her very best by him. She was going to succeed with him—she must! But first of all she must get his co-operation. Was he going to give that easily—or not?

Before she went back to the sickroom she rang up Dr. Beltane's Tulleen number.

He answered the telephone himself, inquired briskly about her journey and when she had arrived, and then said:

'Frankly, I'm glad you're there, Nurse. I think we may see some improvement in the patient now. But I warn you—he may need handling. Part of his difficulty is psychological as much as physical, I suspect. He wants handling. Any difficulties so far?'

'No, none,' hedged Joanna. 'I'm going back to him now—to make him ready for the night.'

'Good. Well, I'll see you in the morning, Nurse. Goodbye.'

She returned to Roger to find that Shuan was no longer with him. He was reading and did not at first look up when she began to move about, doing some deft and unobtrusive tidying of the room.

But when she had finished and turned round to ask him about the making of his bed she found that his eyes were upon her.

She put her question, and he replied laconically:

'Shuan and Cook—being the sturdiest members of the household—usually do it between them. If you yank twice at that bell-rope someone will come.'

He watched her find the bell-rope and pull it. Then he said:

'Don't you think I paved the way rather well—for the ultimate dismissal of Bambina and Co., I mean?'

'If that was your object, I think you did it extraordinarily clumsily,' retorted Joanna briskly. 'You upset Miss Ferrall quite unnecessarily.'

'But you mean them to go, don't you? *Don't* you?' he persisted.

'I certainly don't think that three dogs of that size are suitable as permanent inhabitants of a sick-room,' Joanna admitted. 'But—'

'But you meant to go about their dismissal oh so tactfully and quietly! Almost so that no one would realize they had gone—until they had! But I warned you that you would have to fight Shuan about it—'

'—And proceeded to make quite sure that I should!' put in Joanna imperturbably. 'It doesn't matter about me. I can take care of myself. But you knew Miss Ferrall would be hurt at the suggestion that I—'

Oh, call her Shuan, for goodness' sake!'

'Well, Shuan, then. You knew she wouldn't like the idea. So why did you do it?'

He looked at her oddly. 'Shock tactics—for you!' he said unexpectedly. 'I was having a small bet with myself as to whether, being put to it, you would go all briskly professional and show the courage of your conviction that all that dog was too much of a good thing, or whether you would back down. You backed down, of course. I was disappointed in you.'

'Indeed!' Joanna did not know whether to be annoyed or amused as he went on calmly:

'Yes. And you needn't suppose Shuan would have been really hurt. She would merely have enjoyed a fight. We all do. And in an Irish fight there are no rules of the game!'

Baffled as to how far to take him seriously, Joanna gave it up and was saved from further argument by the appearance at the door of the fat cook who had shown her to her room.

Together they worked at the task of making her patient comfortable for the night, and then Joanna went to her room to change for dinner.

Remembering the chilly atmosphere of the dining-room, she put on a warm dark dress and went downstairs to find that Shuan was there, wearing a grey woollen dress which was too colourless for her and in which she looked gauche and slightly uncomfortable. Mrs. Carnehill had merely discarded the check apron and had the appearance of having powdered her nose too hastily.

She seemed to have recoverd her spirits, and at sight of Joanna she smiled warmly.

'D'you see now,' she asked rhetorically, 'what a help you've been to me already! I've been able to catch up on work which should have been done days ago, and when I looked in on Roger before I came in to dinner he seemed quite cheerful!'

'I'm glad of that,' said Joanna, not without irony.

'Yes. You know, I ought to be frank with you and tell you that when the suggestion of having a nurse for Roger was first mooted by Dr. Beltane and backed up by Colonel Kimstone, I didn't like the idea at all. Maybe I was even a bit jealous at the thought of anyone else—a stranger—helping to look after him! But now I believe it will be good for him to have someone as fresh and young as you are.'

Shuan's head, which had been bent over her soup, came up sharply. Mrs Carnehill looked at her questioningly and then, with a smile, reached over to give the girl's cheek a gentle pinch.

'There, alannah!' she said. 'We know Roger has you too! But between us, we haven't got him to the point where he's able to get about again and so be free of the lot of us. Maybe now, with Joanna to help us, we'll see him improve beyond recognition.'

Mrs. Carnehill changed the subject by asking her ward how she had fared at Naas market.

'Well enough,' returned the girl listlessly. 'I think I remembered everything I went for. And I've sold Bambina's next litter.'

'You have, so? That's grand news. And how much did you spend on the strength of it?' teased Mrs. Carnehill.

'Not too much.' From Shuan's eyes flashed a note of warning which Joanna took to mean that the powderbowl was not to be mentioned. Evidently the gift was to be kept secret.

'I believe we can like each other, she and I,' thought Joanna. 'After all, it isn't *our* fault that we stepped off on the wrong foot almost as soon as we met!'

Mrs. Carnehill turned to Joanna. 'Did you like your room? Do you know, Shuan arranged it all herself?'

'I thought it charming,' said Joanna quietly.

'You'll have to go to Dublin,' Mrs.

Carnehill went on. 'Justin would take you both in his car one day. I wonder what you'll think of the city?' she added. 'We love it, of course.'

They compared cities during the rest of the meal. Then Mrs. Carnehill announced that she was going to spend an hour with Roger.

When she had gone Shuan said ungraciously:

'You didn't say anything about the powderbowl to Mums?'

'No. I didn't think you wanted me to,' said Joanna gently. 'You didn't, did you?'

'No, I didn't.'

After a minute or two's silence Joanna tried again.

'Do you know, I admired my room directly I saw it? I remembered wondering who had arranged it for me. That particular shade of green is so restful.'

There was a pause. Then Shuan said sullenly: 'You don't *have* to be polite about it, you know.'

Taken aback, Joanna still managed to reply gently: 'You mean you didn't do it for me personally, so that there's no need for me to pretend I like it if I don't? But that seems to make you all the more clever—to have arranged a room as tasteful and as pleasing as mine, for someone you'd never seen!'

Shuan, however, would not come even half-way to friendship. She muttered. 'I

31

didn't do it for anyone but Mums—because she wanted me to, and she gave me a free hand. *I* never wanted you, and neither did Roger really. For her own sake Mums pretends that he did, but Roger hates being interfered with and managed. We didn't need you; Roger would have got well without you!'

The childish show of petulance left Joanna almost speechless. But she said coolly: 'Aren't you making a lot of difficulties where they don't exist? *And* magnifying my importance? Of course Mr. Carnehill's recovery doesn't depend on whether I'm here or not! But isn't it—his recovery, I mean—something we can *all* work for and share in when it happens?'

'But it won't! It can't be the same any more!' broke in the girl passionately. 'It will be you who'll take Beltie's orders about Roger; it will be you who will try to rearrange everything about him. Look at the dogs, this afternoon. You must have said something— Roger wouldn't have made it up! I've always heard that about nurses—they never can leave things as they find them. But it won't work with Roger—he hates change, and if you try to force it on him you'll only make an enemy of him in the end!'

'My dear Shuan—I may call you Shuan, mayn't I?—do realize that if I made a habit of making enemies out of my patients, soon I shouldn't have the chance of attending anyone,' Joanna advised dryly. 'I'm just another pair of hands, perhaps a bit more skilled than yours or his mother's. But I *can't* take your place with him—or hers. She realizes that—so why can't you?'

She stopped at sight of the girl's widely staring eyes and rapidly blinking lashes. Shuan said quickly: 'You—oh, you don't *understand*—!' Then, as if afraid of betraying that she was near to tears, she turned and ran out of the room.

Puzzled and dismayed, Joanna sat on alone by the fire until Mrs. Carnehill returned. Soon afterwards she excused herself, saying that she would go to bed. But before she went she said quietly.

'Mr. Carnehill tells me that Shuan usually takes his early tea to him in the mornings. Do you think she would like to go on doing that?'

'Why, yes, I think the child would. If that's all right with you?'

'Yes, of course. I'll leave it to her.' Joanna hesitated, wondering whether she ought to tell Mrs. Carnehill of the hostility which her own arrival had aroused in Shuan. But she decided to say nothing. For all the girl's rudeness, Joanna had a certain sympathy for her; she was, after all, no more than a child who thought herself supplanted. And Joanna believed that she had tact enough to deal with a situation of that sort.

She said good night and went to her room. She undressed quickly, put on a warm house-gown and unpinned the shining knot of her hair. It tumbled slowly in a golden cascade over her shoulders and she began the leisurely ritual of its nightly brushing in long, rhythmical strokes.

When she had finished she took from a compartment in her dressing-case writing materials and the fountain-pen which Dale Woodward had given her for her last birthday.

She began to write:

'My dear Dale—' but there she stopped.

She remembered that this had been going to be a funny letter. That she had been making mental notes all day, meaning, when she wrote it, to recount all the oddities of her first day in Ireland.

But somehow, tonight, none of it seemed very laughable. Overlaid upon it now was a depressing sense of conflict, of difficult situations lying ahead. And she knew that, tonight at any rate, she could not write of Carrieghmere without betraying to Dale that she had misgivings as to her dealings with the people in it.

And Dale had no use or understanding of what he called 'whimsy-whamsies'. As a scientist, he had the scientist's precision of mind. For Dale, in his work of research chemistry, disease was a matter of a germ, a microscope and the intriguing 'isolation' to follow. And he would not try to understand, as Joanna herself must, that strange tempers and incalculable moods were the things which made patients into *people*.

No, Dale would not understand . . . 'If you don't think you can cope, throw up the case and come home'—that was how he would reply bluntly to any doubts she might voice. So, until she could be funny and confident and casual about Carrieghmere, about Roger Carnehill and Shuan Ferrall, she would not write at all.

She poised her pen once more over the paper.

Dear Dale,
This is just to let you know that I arrived safely. I'll tell you all about everything in a day or two. I'm just going to bed! Good night.
Affectionately,
Joanna.

She had never written so briefly to Dale before.

CHAPTER THREE

It was barely light when she awoke next day to wonder what Carrieghmere's early morning routine was.

She had just decided that she would get up when there was a knock at the door, and a girl in a pink print dress, over which she wore a green cardigan and an apron of doubtful whiteness, came in.

Roseen, yesterday's absent housemaid, decided Joanna, as the tea-tray was brought to her bedside.

She smiled as she sat up. 'Thank you. I didn't expect this. I wonder if you would draw the curtains before you go?'

But Roseen was staring at her, apparently entranced. When she moved over to the window she did so by backing away from the bed, still gazing dumbly at Joanna.

At last she said in a rich Connemara brogue: 'I wasn't expecting to see anyone of the likes of you! 'Tis middle-aged and crabby I thought you'd be. And you with the fair looks of one of them models! Your hair, now!'

Amused and slightly embarrassed by this outburst, Joanna shook back her hair and looked up at the girl with a twinkle in her eye.

'You're Roseen, aren't you? You wouldn't have been kissing your famous Blarney stone, by any chance?'

Roseen took the accusation without humour. 'I have not, so!' she declared indignantly. ''Twas surprise alone that took my manner away from me for the moment.'

She put her head on one side as she continued to eye Joanna speculatively. 'Now 'tis my own deep ambition to be a nurse, but I'm not let to go to England alone.'

'What about Dublin?' put in Joanna.

'Nor to Dublin, till the day I'll be twenty-one. My mother says—But you'll be wanting your tea, miss. I'll leave you now—'

She began to back towards the door, but Joanna stopped her to ask:

'What about Mr. Roger's tea? Has Miss Shuan taken it to him yet?'

Roseen looked faintly astonished. 'Mr. Roger's tea, is it? Miss Shuan won't be at that for an hour or more!'

Joanna glanced at her travelling clock. 'But I understood Mr. Roger to say that she took it to him at about seven?'

'Arrah, no. 'Tis nearer eight and oftener nine when Miss Shuan does be getting it for him! What for would he be wanting it earlier, and him lying there all day, the way time would be nothing to him at all?'

The girl went out, and Joanna leaned over to pour a well-stewed brew into a cup of equally exquisite fineness as the china from which she had lunched and dined yesterday. What a very odd household this was, to be sure, she thought.

Then she bathed and dressed and twisted her hair into its familiar neat knot beneath the cap of her uniform.

She went briskly down to the kitchen to find that she was expected to use for her patient the contents of a large earthenware teapot standing on the hearth before the peat fire.

'I think,' said Joanna with the firm gentleness with which she usually got her way, 'it would be better if we made some fresh tea.'

At this the fat woman known as Cook looked truculent, and Roseen ventured:

'Mr. Roger likes his tea strong.'

'Maybe. But I'd still like him to have it newly made. Do you mind—?'

The cool confidence in her voice sent Cook, muttering slightly, to fill another kettle while Roseen prepared a tray. When it was ready she took it to Roger Carnehill's room, to find that he was already awake.

'Good morning,' said Joanna.

'Good morning.' He frowned slightly. 'Where's Shuan?' he demanded.

'I don't think she's up yet.' Joanna's voice was equable as she set down the tray. 'So, as you said you usually waked at seven or so, I brought your tea myself.'

He regarded her with the rather inscrutable amusement to which she told herself she must get used.

'Yesterday,' he remarked dispassionately, 'you were ready to accuse me of deliberately creating difficulties between you and Shuan.

38

Aren't you beginning to wield a very pretty new broom in the child's face yourself? She's awfully jealous of her "privileges". And she regards the bringing of my tea as one of the most important of them.'

'But they tell me in the kitchen that often you don't get it until between eight and nine—'

'Well, what of it? There's time enough—'

'Not,' retorted Joanna crisply, 'on a morning when I'm expecting my first visit from your doctor. Do you mind—?' Again it was the cool assurance that she would be obeyed which constrained Roger to take from her the proffered teacup.

He gulped its contents and looked up with a grimace. 'What have they made this from? Last night's washing-up water?'

'I had it freshly made. I thought you would prefer it.'

'But we *like* our tea with a bit of body to it! You're not going to anglicize that! Take it away. I can't drink it.'

He set down the cup petulantly. After a second's hesitation Joanna, her fair skin flushed with annoyance at his rudeness, picked up the tray and moved towards the door. But before she reached it a voice from the bed said:

'I'm sorry. You couldn't know. I'll have a stab at it if you like.' He beckoned rather imperiously towards the tray, and so she

39

brought it back to him.

She had left his room and was crossing the hall when the baize door leading to the kitchen regions was flung open as three lumbering golden bodies jostled each other for place. They were followed by Shuan, who held their leashes gathered into one hand, while she held her dressing gown from her feet with the other.

Her lovely eyes were bright with the hurt indignation of a child as, at sight of Joanna, she accused:

'You've taken Roger's tea! I *always* do it! And Mums told you she wanted me to go on. I know she did, because I asked her after you'd gone to bed. You haven't any right to interfere like this!'

Rather pointedly—perhaps even a little cruelly, she thought afterwards—Joanna glanced at her watch. 'I'm sorry,' she said. '*I* asked Mrs. Carnehill whether you would like to go on as before. But Dr. Beltane is coming this morning, and it is getting late—'

'Late! As though Beltie cares, so long as he can get asked to lunch! Why, it isn't half-past eight! And Roger hates being dragged out of sleep just for *tea!*'

'He was already awake,' Joanna pointed out dryly. Then she went on more gently: 'But does it really matter who takes his tea? He's still drinking it. Why don't you take the dogs in and talk to him as you usually do, until I'm

40

ready to give him his blanket bath?'

Shuan stared, hostility mixed with incredulity in her eyes. 'You don't really want the dogs in Roger's room. He said you didn't.'

'It's a matter of entire indifference to me, until I've had the doctor's orders to the contrary.' Joanna felt suddenly that, given a little more provocation, she might smack Shuan—quite pleasurably.

'Well, you won't get those. Beltie doesn't care what we do so long as we keep Roger happy.' And Shuan swept on across the hall towards Roger's room.

As Joanna went about her work her feeling alternated between extreme irritation and an odd sympathy for Shuan. She began to wonder, too, what sort of an ally this 'Beltie'—Dr. Beltane—would prove to be. On the telephone she had liked the sound of his voice, but Shuan seemed to set such store by his authority that she had already begun to feel prejudiced against him.

At breakfast Mrs. Carnehill announced that she must go to Dublin, but that Beltie was to be duly invited to lunch if he wanted to stay.

'He'll want to,' interposed Shuan.

'Yes. He usually does,' replied Mrs. Carnehill placidly. 'Though I've never known, really, how he has the time—'

'What time may I expect him?' asked Joanna.

41

'Oh, say about eleven. Maybe later. Shuan dear, Justin is coming to dinner tonight—did I tell you? I forgot I was going to Dublin, but I dare say I shall be back.'

'Is René coming too?' inquired Shuan.

'Well, I didn't ask him particularly, but if he does, be nice to him, there's a good girl.' Mrs. Carnehill turned to Joanna. 'You've met Justin McKiley; René Menden is a young Belgian who is studying farming on the estate,' she explained. 'He is living with Mr. McKiley at the Dower House—'

'—When he isn't living here,' put in Shuan pertly.

'Shuan, that's not fair! He very rarely comes here unless he is asked. And his manners are charming—'

'He *goggles* so! He clicks his heels when he bows, and he wanted to kiss my hand!' objected Shuan.

'Well, you can hardly measure his behaviour alongside that of the corner-boys of Tulleen!' was Mrs. Carnehill's dry comment. 'You're not very tolerant, are you, alannah?' she added more indulgently as she saw from the girl's face that the rebuke had been taken.

It was a little later, when she was searching—rather hopelessly—through the papers on her desk for some details of Roger's hospital treatment required by Joanna, that Mrs. Carnehill said reflectively:

'D'you know, I think young Menden

believes he is in love with Shuan.'

'In love?' echoed Joanna. 'But she's only a child!'

Mrs. Carnehill looked over her shoulder to give her gentle smile. 'She is eighteen. And wasn't I married myself within a year of the selfsame age?'

'She doesn't love him?' Joanna put the question while she tried to assimilate this new idea about Shuan. Certainly she found it difficult to associate with her any emotion as mature as—love!

'No, I'm sure not. And I don't think it has occurred to her that his "goggling," as she calls it, is part of his complaint. I can only hope that she won't hurt him too much, unwittingly.'

Joanna said carefully: 'She is very devoted to Mr. Carnehill, isn't she?'

'Why, yes. And I've been so grateful for it. But now she ought to get out and about more. I confess I'd like to see her considering the possibilities of René as a companion—'

'She doesn't seem anxious for freedom. She's very single-minded,' murmured Joanna.

'Single-minded—in her devotion to Roger, you mean? Yes, I know.' Mrs. Carnehill smiled a little sadly. 'Why, she sometimes finds it necessary to protect him even from *me*!'

Her bright eyes clouded as they had done

43

yesterday and Joanna, herself understanding very little of the cause of the conflict between her patient and his mother, thought it best to make no direct comment. Instead she held out her hand to take the medical notes which her employer had just unearthed, as she said gently:

'Shuan is very young. And as intolerant as youth itself. Perhaps one ought to remember that.'

Mrs. Carnehill smiled. 'You talk as if your own youth weren't still in a cloud about you, my dear!' she chided. 'And you at the very age to be my own daughter, if I had one!'

Then, tacitly, the subject was dismissed. From then on, until Mrs. Carnehill's final departure by car for Tulleen station, the preparations for the journey took on a kind of crescendo of flurry.

As the car disappeared down the weedy drive Shuan turned away, saying ungraciously: 'I'm going to exercise the dogs.'

Joanna watched her go, thinking that she must take her own advice by being as tolerant as possible of the girl's gaucherie. She remembered Shuan's passionate exclamation of last night. What was it, Joanna wondered, that she did not understand?

At about noon Dr. Beltane arrived. He drove a battered-looking car up the drive and walked without ceremony into the house and into his patient's room.

44

Joanna's first impression of him was one of *roundness*—a sort of Pickwickian roundness of face and body and legs. His bedside manner was of a hearty variety, and she thought that Roger Carnehill did not respond very graciously to it. But she herself liked him and felt reassured that she would be able to work under his authority.

He examined and questioned Roger and said at last:

'Well, I saw your surgeon the other day, and we shall be trying the light treatment again soon.'

'That means Dublin again, I suppose?' asked Roger wearily. 'It didn't do any good last time.

'Well, last time isn't this time,' retorted Dr. Beltane rather obviously. 'Why approach it in that spirit? You try a bit of co-operation for a change, Roger me lad. You'd be surprised at the good it'd do you. You surely don't want Nurse Merivale here to go back to England, saying that we have no surgery that's worth the blade of a scalpel in Eire? You'd not put us to that shame!'

Roger shrugged indifferently. He watched the doctor pack his instruments and then asked: 'How's the car?'

Dr. Beltane gave a start of feigned surprise. 'Well, now isn't it the odd thing that you should ask! It went fine after your Michael passed his hand over it, the last time I was out. But it's not running so well now.'

Roger regarded the ceiling.

'You mean you might bring yourself to stay to lunch while Michael had another look at it?'

Dr. Beltane beamed rosily. 'That'd be putting Mrs. Carnehill to too much trouble—' he began. But Roger interposed:

'You old wretch, you know you hoped to be asked! Besides, Mother is in Dublin. You'll lunch with Shuan and—Joanna.'

The doctor glanced quickly in Joanna's direction as he beckoned to her to leave the room with him.

Outside he said conversationally: 'Michael is a stable lad here—with his heart in mechanics, though his job is with horses. He understands my car far better than my own man does. Now, Nurse, I'd like a word with you.'

'Yes, Doctor.' Joanna hesitated. 'Perhaps I ought to explain about Mr. Carnehill's using my Christian name. If you don't approve—'

'Ah, think nothing of it. The lad won't respond to starchiness. We've got to cut across this barrier of apathy that he is setting up increasingly as we don't see much progress in the lifting of this partial paralysis of his lower spine. We'll get at it yet. But he won't believe that. He needs a bit of jollying out of the moods—the self-pity—that he gets into.'

Joanne smiled demurely. 'Do you

46

recommend that *I* try "jollying"?'

'Well, you saw me, Nurse. A bit of healthy ridicule will do no harm. Part of his trouble is that he's fairly *cluttered* by devotion—'

'You mean Mrs. Carnehill and—Miss Ferrall?'

'Yes, and about Mrs. Carnehill, frankly, I don't understand her treatment of the boy lately. He lies there, pining for news of the estate—how it's going and so forth, market prices and all that—and she pursues a policy of keeping everything from him—"in case he worries"!'

'That's not very wise, surely?' suggested Joanna.

'So I tell her. But the good woman is as obstinate as—as a Carnehill. And that's saying something, for of course she wasn't born one. She shuts up like an oyster and says she won't take things to him until he's better—much better. She won't accept my word that she's slowly starving him of something which was once his whole life's interest. Perhaps you could watch your chance, Nurse, and say a word about that too?'

'I'll try,' promised Joanna, though a trifle doubtfully. She wondered whether the doctor knew about that other source of annoyance to Roger—Mrs. Carnehill's work. But she supposed he did, since he seemed to know the family very well.

47

Meanwhile she was glad that she would have his company at lunch—she hadn't been looking forward to a meal alone with Shuan!

When she went in to Roger in the afternoon he said abruptly:

'McKiley is coming to dinner. If Mother isn't back, will you see that he comes to me afterwards?'

There was an imperious arrogance in his tone, and after a pause he inquired:

'You've met McKiley. What do you think of him?'

Joanna looked her surprise. 'Why, I hardly know. He was very kind—'

'M'm. Gallantry becomes him. But surely—your first real contact in this country, and no first impressions?' Again the blue eyes were veiled with amusement.

Joanna smiled. 'Well, nothing particularly lasting, I think. He invited me to go and see the Dower House one day, I remember.'

Roger frowned. 'Damned impertinence! Why didn't you snub him?'

An imp of mischief entered Joanna. 'Perhaps,' she said carefully, 'because I didn't know then how much he was in need of recreation. Safety first!'

'Well, do you know now?' He sounded offended, and she realized that her joke had not been too well taken. She said quickly: 'I'm sorry, I oughtn't to have said that. It sounded—'

'—Coy and unexpectedly cheap, I thought! But I suppose you're right. You've got to keep something in reserve for yourself, to prevent people like us from thinking that we've hired more of you than your services. I daresay you've even got a private life of your own, over there in England?'

'I daresay.' Joanna's tone was dry. 'Most people have, haven't they?'

'Er—family—and all that?'

'My people are dead.'

'Habitat?'

'London.'

'Hobbies? Recreations?'

Joanna laughed. 'Oh, the usual feminine variety. Not very interesting ones.'

'Evidently you've been taught not to confide in strangers! How long must you know me before it will be proper to mention what an orphan nurse in London does with her spare time?'

'I'd willingly tell you now, if I thought you'd be interested. But you wouldn't be,' she remarked.

'No, perhaps not.' He stretched his arm rather wearily above his head and appeared, in a way that was characteristic of him, to have lost all interest in the conversation. He said suddenly:

'By the way, the dogs haven't been in here since morning. Does that represent a moral victory for you—or a gathering of the storm?'

49

Joanna paused on her way to the door. 'Neither, I hope,' she said quietly. 'I don't want to quarrel with Shuan. Please don't make me think it's inevitable!'

He laughed. 'My dear Joanna, as if you or I have any say in the inevitability of *that*!'

By some incalculable caprice of the kitchen, dinner was served early that evening, and between seeing to Roger's own meal and appearing in the dining-room Joanna had no time to change out of uniform.

Justin McKiley took her hand, and smiled as if there were some secret alliance between them. René Menden, the young Belgian, slim, upright and with darkly polished hair, bowed stiffly and said:

'I have not been invited to dinner, but Mr. McKiley has said that I am ever welcome, he is sure. Correct my verbs, please?'

He spoke to Joanna, but his glance was for Shuan, who repeated mechanically: 'I wasn't invited, but Mr. McKiley said I should always be welcome.'

René smiled gratefully at her. 'Ah, yes. I have forgotten.'

'I forgot,' corrected Shuan again, this time sounding bored.

At dinner Joanna watched them interestedly. It was plain that Mrs. Carnehill was right and that René had no eyes for anyone but Shuan. She snubbed him or ignored him or corrected his English with a bored, patient disinterest which, in his place, Joanna felt she would have resented. She was glad when, at the end of the meal, he persuaded her to take him to find a book he was going to borrow.

Joanna said to Justin McKiley: 'Mr. Carnehill told me to ask you to go and see him after dinner.'

He stirred his coffee and did not move. 'Ah, time enough,' he said indifferently.

Joanna stood up. 'Then I'd better go back to him—'

'What's the hurry? I'm going to see him in a minute. Take your coffee with me at least?'

Reluctantly Joanna sat down again. She could hardly do otherwise, though she felt that by doing so she was helping him to prolong that elusive minute.

He said abruptly: 'The Americans have a word for it, I believe.'

Joanna looked her bewilderment.

'Rooting, I think they call it. At dinner you were rooting hard for young René—digging your nails into your palms with anxiety for him! You are just like Mrs. Carnehill—ready to spread your wings over him to save him from Shuan's brutality!'

'I thought she was almost rude to him, once or twice,' replied Joanna rather coolly.

'Well, you'll agree that the young fool asks for it! Let him fight his own battles. In any case, surely you're too young and—too lovely,

51

if that isn't forward of me!—to adopt this mothering attitude! Or does it'—again his glance appraised her—'come with the uniform, so to speak?'

'I don't think I know what you mean?'

'Don't you?' His smile flashed at her. 'Come now, do you mean to tell me that you've never been tempted to play a part which you felt was becoming to your uniform?'

'I don't think so. I—'

'Nor sheltered behind it? Retired into the cold impersonality of it, in order to get yourself out of a difficult situation? Nor, conversely, used the damned attractiveness of it for your own ends?'

Joanna said evenly: 'If I did any of those things, wouldn't that make me a very artificial person?'

His eyes mocked her. 'No. Merely a woman! And a woman must make her own armour—as she must make her own weapons. I've always supposed that a pretty nurse could use her uniform as either—on occasion.'

Joanna rose abruptly. This foolish conversation had gone far enough. 'Hadn't you better go to Mr. Carnehill now?' she inquired coolly.

He had risen too. 'I suppose so,' he said as they moved towards the door together. For an instant he laid a hand lightly upon her arm.

'You'll remember our pact? That you will

come to the Dower House when things get too much for you here?'

'Why should they ever do that?'

He shrugged. 'Maybe they won't. In that case, I should regard your visit merely as a formal call. But I think you will come.'

To her chagrin, Joanna found no adequate reply to the cool effrontery of this assumption. As she hesitated, the door opened and Mrs. Carnehill came in.

'Ah, there you are, Justin,' she said. 'I'm sorry, I was kept later than I expected in the city. You've had your dinner? Have you seen Roger?'

'On my way now. Miss Merivale and I have been keeping each other company over our coffee.'

'Well, do go to Roger. He was rather insistent. But don't quote more figures at him than you can help. He worries so—'

Justin spread his hands in a gesture which seemed to reassure her. 'I can't quote figures. I haven't any with me. Just an overall picture of how things are going—that's all he wants?'

'I—think so.' She watched him nervously as he left the room. Then she turned to Joanna. 'They don't care for each other, those two. But *you* liked Justin—didn't you?'

It was a question which Joanna had already asked herself. But so far she had not found the answer.

CHAPTER FOUR

During the next few days Joanna was to realize that, until then, she had seen nothing which could be described as one of Roger's 'black moods.' For, of the depth of depression into which he was plunged after his interview with Justin, there could be no doubt.

But at Joanna's suggestion that he was bored, Mrs. Carnehill looked doubtful. 'Do you think so now? But why would he be bored? Haven't we all got our brains fairly wracked out, thinking of diversions for him? And nearly always he has someone with him!'

Joanna felt she began to understand what the doctor had meant when he said Roger was being 'smothered' by devotion. She said carefully: 'I didn't mean amusements or company, so much as exercise for his mind. Wouldn't it be possible for him to take some share in the running of the estate? I understand he used to do it all, with Mr. McKiley's help. Mustn't he feel completely at a loss, without some responsibility for it?'

It was as if a curtain had been drawn guardedly across her companion's face. She spoke more shortly than she had yet done to Joanna. 'He's not fit for it. I told you, he and Justin don't care for each other. And having

54

to concern himself with the estate only worries him.'

Joanna gave it up. But she could not agree with her employer.

She was wondering how she could help him when he suddenly broached the subject himself.

'I wish *you'd* get some figures out of somebody,' he growled. 'I've struggled long enough against this conspiracy of silence Mother has set up. Ask René Menden—he ought to have some idea by now of what goes on.'

'But—'

He looked at her with a kind of cold contempt.

'So you're a party to it too? Or else you're going to say primly "How can I go behind Mr. McKiley's back?" All right, don't bother.'

'I wasn't going to say anything of the sort,' retorted Joanna. 'I was merely going to point out that I've met your student only once, that I don't know where to find him during his working day and that I've no idea what you want to know.'

'Well, I want to know the real figures of the stock that went to the market last month, for instance. And what price it fetched. I can get from the papers what the market price was, but did we get it? That's what I can't get out of that evasive fool, McKiley. And I want the milking figures and the egg returns—'

'But is René Menden likely to know all that?' asked Joanna dubiously.

Roger gestured helplessly. 'No, probably not. Perhaps I've never expected that he would.'

'Well, I could ask him,' said Joanna quickly.

'M'm. I suppose you couldn't get less than McKiley's "satisfactory" and "measuring up pretty well by last year's standard!" As for Menden, he's at the Dower House. But I suppose you knew that?'

'Yes. But I couldn't go there to see him. It's Mr. McKiley's house.'

'It isn't. It's ours,' commented Roger aloofly.

It was the sort of childish quibble which she would have expected from Shuan. In their inability to see anybody's point but their own they were rather alike, these two, reflected Joanna.

'Well, it still wouldn't be politic to pump René Mendon on Mr. McKiley's doorstep, would it?' she responded equably.

At that he rounded upon her irritably. 'Good heavens, woman, do you think I'm asking you to enter into a *conspiracy* to get facts about my own property? As if I care for McKiley!'

'I was thinking that it wouldn't make for easier relations with him,' Joanna pointed out. 'And Mrs. Carnehill says you can't do without him.'

'Oh, Mother—! She's unknowable lately. All this frantic journalism, all this keeping of "worry" from me. What is she afraid of, anyway? *You'd* say she was afraid of something, wouldn't you?'

'What makes you think that?' Joanna's tone was guarded.

'Ah, don't hedge! Isn't it staring you in the face? She believes that—that there's no cure for me. And she tells herself that she's "facing facts". It's something that Carnehills have to drive themselves to!'

Joanna said quietly: 'That's nonsense, and you know it. Your cure is only a matter of time. And Mrs. Carnehill likes her work too well to give it up. If she's afraid of anything—'

'Well, she is, isn't she?'

'—it's that *when* you are well again, she won't be able to continue her journalism on the scale to which she is developing it now.'

He looked at her with his disturbing perception. 'Diplomatically turned. But not terribly convincing, my dear Joanna,' he remarked coolly.

She felt desperately sorry for him, knowing that at present he had no power within himself to combat his destructive self-pity. She longed to be able to give him some of her own strength of conviction that he would get well. But so far he would give her no clue as to how to reach him. She wished, for one thing, that when he first suggested that Mrs. Carnehill was afraid, she had rejected the idea at once with hearty scorn. That he was wrong, Joanna was certain. But that Mrs. Carnehill was indeed 'afraid of something' she was almost equally sure.

Before she left him she asked lightly: 'Well, shall I speak to René Menden?'

But he had apparently already lost interest. 'Oh, do as you please. You'll not learn much, I dare say.'

More than once during that week Joanna remembered guiltily that she had not sent her promised second letter to Dale. But she did not realize that he would worry at the absence of news from her until one morning when the solitary letter on her tray was a confirmatory telegram.

She tore it open while Roseen watched with interest.

She read—

'Deeply worried no further letter. Are you all right, dear? Reply. Dale.'

The reply had been paid and a glance showed that the original had been handed in in London early on the previous morning. Joanna looked up at Roseen.

'There should have been a telegram for me yesterday—by telephone, I suppose. Do you know anything about one?'

'A telegram, is it? Sure, and wasn't Miss Shuan at the phone yesterday forenoon while you were with Mr. Roger?'

'I don't know. Was she? It could have been an ordinary message she was taking. Did she say anything about a telegram for me?'

'Divil a word. Was it urgent news, now?' inquired Roseen with compassionate interest. 'Will I hunt Miss Shuan to you as soon as she is up?'

'You needn't bother to hunt her anywhere. I'll ask her about it when I see her.' And Joanna dressed hastily, trying as she did so to calculate how long her belated reply to Dale would take to reach London.

When, later, she confronted Shuan with the confirmatory wire the girl took refuge in a sullen defiance.

'Yes, I took it over the phone,' she admitted. 'It came about eleven.'

'Well, haven't you any method for dealing with messages and wires? Couldn't you have written it down?' Joanna felt baffled.

'There isn't any paper, and Roseen is always borrowing the pencil. I would have told you, only you were in Roger's room and you're always so fussy about being interrupted—'

'Only because I want a certain amount of privacy for him when I'm doing anything for him. Anyway, you could have told me as soon as I was free.'

'Well, I forgot. If it was terribly urgent, I'm sorry.'

'You know what it said, so you must know that it wasn't terribly urgent. But it *was*—worrying,' commented Joanna dryly.

She was prepared to leave the matter there, but to her surprise and annoyance she found that when she next went to him, Roger had heard all about the incident.

He said with reasonable cheerfulness: 'I've given Shuan a good moral belting for you! She won't do it again.'

'Do what—oh, did she tell you about the telegram?' Joanna flushed. 'It was all very trivial really.'

'She didn't want to tell me. But she came in here with a face like a storm over the Wicklows, and I wormed it out of her,' said Roger with relish. The blue eyes challenged hers. 'Why *hadn't* you given the young man news of yourself?'

'I've been too busy to write.' She felt annoyed that the contents of the wire as well as the incident had been discussed, but she would not show irritation if she could help it.

There was a pause while his eyes remained fixed upon her, as if he expected her to go on. When she did not he asked:

'Well, don't you *mind* that Shuan told me the wording? Aren't you going off the deep end about "private correspondence"—and all that?'

60

'A telephoned telegram is hardly private correspondence, is it? I couldn't complain if the whole of Tulleen knew what it contained!'

'No, but—well, hang it, haven't you a grouse at all?'

Joanna laughed. 'You sound as if you want me to have one. All right. I *was* annoyed—'

'Come, that's human of you!' He seemed relieved as he regarded her shrewdly beneath lowered lids. 'You're annoyed—aren't you?—because you think I've been let in on a scrap of that private life of yours that you were so starchy about keeping from me the other day?'

'No, of course not. And I wasn't starchy. It was simply that I felt you couldn't be interested in gossip about what I do with my time in London.'

'But I could be!' He was serious now. He put out a hand to take her wrist in a grip which hurt. 'I *wanted* you to talk the other day. Not because I'm nosy or curious, but because I've *got* to make myself remember that there's a world outside all this.' His eyes swept from cornice to floor and from wall to confining wall of the room. 'Don't you see how easy, how damnably easy it is to forget? And that everyone here seems intent on making me believe that *this* is my whole future?'

Joanna gently disengaged her wrist and wished she hadn't when he looked rebuffed.

'I do understand,' she said, pitying him. 'But you're wrong when you think no one helps you to get outside it. *You* don't always help yourself, you know!'

'Don't I know it? It's a kind of black despair that grips me. Sometimes—do you know, Joanna?—I even *use* it against them to pay them out for—for *swaddling* me here!'

'You use it against yourself more.' Her tone held a quiet conviction which seemed to impress him.

'I know that too. But it's the only rebellion I've got to my hand, do you see?' He relaxed slightly and gave her a wry smile. 'I'd use it against you too—only you don't seem to mind. It's your English imperturbability, I suppose.'

'Well, don't trade on it too much,' warned Joanna, smiling. 'Even English worms will turn!' Suddenly she felt happy, as if she saw a way to help him opening out before her. Somehow, by talk about herself, by bringing him news of his own estate, by encouraging him to tell her about his life before his accident, she would try to give back to him a belief in a future which lay beyond the confines of this room.

He was saying: 'Well, now you know something of the black devils I contend with. Do you have any of your own?'

'I don't think so.'

'You're—happy?'

'Mostly—yes.'

'I suppose the young man helps. Are you going to marry him?'

Joanna, taken aback by the question, said nothing, and he repeated like an importunate child: 'Well, are you?'

'He hasn't asked me.'

'You know that's hedging. And no answer to what I asked.'

There was nothing but to be frank with him. She said slowly: 'You see, I've known Dale for a very long time. He's a research chemist; when I'm in London we go about together and—and perhaps we've always supposed that—'

'—That when he makes up his mind, you'll be nice and handy, and then he'll pop you into a box of a house in the suburbs and you'll see him off on the eight-fifteen every morning of your lives!'

'Well, doesn't that sound like the happy ending?'

His words were cynical, but Joanna was thankful that his eyes were brighter and she believed that the 'black mood' of the past few days was passing. If only she could keep him like that! But she would, she would!

When she left him she wondered at the ease with which she had been so frank with him about Dale. With the beginnings of a new letter to Dale before her she sat staring at the paper for a long time. From anyone else she would have resented the question as to what her relation to him was. Yet to Roger Carnehill she had expressed quite easily the doubt that was half a conviction—the belief, shared, she thought, by Dale, that one day before long they would marry.

It was a warm, comfortable idea, she had always thought—the knowledge that there was someone with whom you could get on as placidly and agreeably as she and Dale did. It was a better basis for marriage than many people had. And yet—the flash of doubt utterly startled her—hadn't they, so far, missed the love that wrung the heart-strings, stirred the blood? Did she or Dale know anything of the pain and mystery of ecstasy—the flinging of the spirit to the mountain-tops, the plunging to the depths?

Foolish. She chided herself. They were adults, weren't they? Not children crying for the stars!

Joanna picked up her pen and turned her mind resolutely to the matter in hand. Her mind—but not her heart, which cried, childishly and inconsequentially, for the unknown star which had not yet dawned for her...

Then, in the midst of wintry storms, there came a 'gift' of a day of sun and warm wind, and Colonel Kimstone with his wife drove over to see Roger.

'There, Nurse Merivale, we heard you were

here!' said the Colonel, greeting her warmly. He turned to Mrs. Kimstone with an air of Joanna's being his own invention. 'Didn't I say now,' he demanded, 'that this was the very thing for Roger?'

Mrs. Kimstone, a short, button-eyed woman whom Joanna had not met while she had been nursing the Colonel in London, pursed her lips and nodded twice, though Joanna thought her appraising glance was a little doubtful.

'I think I'd been expecting someone *older*,' she said.

'Nonsense! There are no old nurses—they all get married before that, eh, Roger?' exclaimed the Colonel, roaring with laughter at his own quip. Then he said briskly: 'Now we'll take care of the patient, Nurse. Off you go and get some rare sunshine into you.'

Joanna, who had been longing wistfully for some air, accepted her freedom gratefully. She hurried to her room, changed into jeans and a thick sweater, and set off for a tramp round the park, which would mean about two miles of ground new to her.

Towards the end of her walk, she came to the weed-ridden drive leading down to the main gateway and turned up it towards the house. But before she reached it curiosity took her over a narrow path to the right, in order to look at the Dower House where McKiley and the Belgian farm student lived

65

together.

It was small, of the Georgian period, with a slate roof and characteristic windows; it was more homely looking and seemed to be in better repair than Carrieghmere itself. Joanna was just about to turn away, remembering how she had told Roger that she could not question René Menden 'on Mr. McKiley's doorstep,' when someone came up behind her and she turned about to see it was young Menden himself.

He clicked his heels and bowed formally, though he was in working clothes. 'Mademoiselle Merivale? You wish to visit us?'

'No, not really. I only came over to look at the house—'

'But you will come in? In this country they have not—' he corrected himself carefully—'do not have—the custom of the five o'clock tea, *but* Madame 'Agerty know I find her potato-cakes delicious, and at about this hour they often await me. You will share them with me, no?'

'Well, just for a minute.' Joanna's healthy appetite, stimulated by her walk, was registering considerable interest in the matter of potato-cakes. Besides, her curiosity about Justin McKiley extended to the house where he lived and this was her opportunity to see it.

René Menden stood aside as she passed

into the hall. Then he called down a flight of basement stairs: 'Aggy, my cabbage!' and the fat Irishwoman whom Joanna knew to be Mrs. Hagerty, Justin McKiley's housekeeper, came hurrying up the stairs, wiping her hands on her apron as she came.

'Now, Menden,' she said, pronouncing each syllable to rhyme with "ten", 'ye've no call to be addressin' a Christian woman by thim vegetable names. What is it ye want, now?'

René spread his hands. 'But potato-cakes, surely? and perhaps tea for Mademoiselle Merivale?'

'There's no tea but what I had to me dinner. There'd be a lick of it left—'

Joanna shuddered. 'Not for me,' she said hastily. 'A—a glass of milk will do.'

'*Alors*! Milk and potato-cakes, very hot!' ordered René. He turned to Joanna. 'This way. It is here that we eat.'

He led the way into a room off the hall, where a small peat fire burned in the grate and where the tablecloth had an air of being more or less permanently laid.

René explained: 'We are not much here, McKiley and I, after the morning. And he has his own room over there.'

He nodded across the hall to a closed door. 'It is there that he does a great deal of his work, sees his friends, has parties.'

'And you—what about your friends?' put

67

in Joanna gently.

The boy looked startled. 'I? But in Ireland I have no friends. Here I am the stranger, Mademoiselle Merivale!' He spoke without a trace of self-pity, but Joanna felt as sorry for him, the alien, as she did for the ancient grace of the house which, so far as she could see, had been betrayed into dinginess.

She said slowly: 'For you then, Ireland is no more than a—a kind of corridor in your life?' She was thinking that for her, when her work with Roger Carnehill was done, her stay here would appear as no more than that—a passage between one part of her life and the next.

But René was shaking his head. 'No. It is more than that. I shall stay here for a time, learn my work and then go home. But when I return to Belgium I shall at least take memories—perhaps even something more!'

They looked at each other, both knowing that he was speaking of Shuan. Then the boy laughed and made a gesture towards the drab room. 'It is terrible, this, but for me it will not be for ever.' He turned about to take from Mrs. Hagerty a tray containing a jug, two tumblers and a dish of potato-scones. Then he and Joanna sat at adjacent sides of the table and fell to upon the impromptu meal.

'This,' commented René between munches, 'is—as you would say—"fun".'

'Yes, isn't it?' Joanna picked up her glass

confidently, then after the first mouthful, choked and set it down hastily.

'What—?' began René, then burst out laughing. 'Ah, it is *lait-du-buerre*—the buttermilk! I always have it. Do you not like it?'

Joanna grimaced. 'I'm sorry—not a bit!'

'You do not have it in England?'

'No—I suppose we don't make enough butter!'

'That,' said René gallantly, 'I find it difficult to believe. For it is the buttermilk which gives the exquisite complexion, and yours, mademoiselle—!'

Then, laughing, he picked up the jug and Joanna heard him clatter down the stairs to the kitchen.

She glanced at her watch. Soon she must go back to relieve Colonel and Mrs. Kimstone. But just then there was a sound in the hall and Justin McKiley appeared at the open door of the room. With legs apart he stood regarding her, while he bent a riding crop bow-wise between his hands.

He said: 'So you came to find me after all! Didn't I suggest that you would?'

CHAPTER FIVE

Joanna said coolly: 'I was out for a walk and I came to look at the outside of the Dower House. René met me and invited me in to share potato-cakes with him.'

Justin McKiley glanced distastefully at the half-laid table. 'To share also, I see, the squalor of the dining arrangements imposed on us by Mrs. Hagerty. Come to my room, and I'll see that you get tea, properly served, English fashion.'

'No, I can't stay,' Joanna told him. 'René has gone to get some fresh milk, because I can't drink buttermilk. When he comes back I must finish my scones and go.'

'But you'll come again. Having once escaped from bondage, you'll repeat the experience?'

'I have time off regularly every day,' lied Joanna. 'I don't feel in need of any really dramatic "escape".'

'No? Where did you go for your walk?' His tone held only a careless interest.

'Across the park. What a wealth of lovely old trees!'

'M'm. Too many. For too long the Carnehills have pursued a policy of "The timber of Carrieghmere is not for sale." I'm remedying that.'

'So I saw,' commented Joanna dryly.

'You noticed the felling we're doing over by the east wall? Obviously it was criminal to keep it, considering the price timber is fetching.'

'Does Mr. Carnehill approve?' Joanna heard herself asking.

Justin McKiley looked at her quizzically. 'Are you taking me to task?' he inquired amusedly.

'No, only—' Joanna was uncomfortably aware that she was launched upon something which she had not set out to do and for which Roger, particularly, would despise her. She was appealing for him to his agent with whom he had no sympathy.

'Only what?'

'Well, he isn't told enough of what is going on. I'm his nurse and I believe it would help towards his recovery. Dr. Beltane thinks so too. You and Mrs. Carnehill tell him just so much and not enough. He wants details, figures—'

'And he sent you to get them from me—unofficially, of course?'

'*No!*' The denial was indignant. 'My conviction about it is—is professional. After all, he's no child—he's a man—even if he is a sick one!'

'And a sick man appeals to the emotions?' put in McKiley quickly. 'Well, I'm sorry, but it's by Mrs. Carnehill's wish that he isn't

71

worried about the estate.'

'But isn't there *some* department which he could take over, feel himself responsible for?' persisted Joanna. '*You* could convince Mrs. Carnehill of that, surely?'

'And force him into feeling that he is the child you claim he isn't? "Here, Roger dear, is a teeny-weeny duty that's all your own"—how do you suppose he'd react to that? No, the overall, general picture is best—'

It was a shrewd point, but Joanna did not feel convinced. However, as she was about to reply, René came back with the milk, and she had to swallow a glassful hastily as she finished her scone.

She said to him: 'I must go. Thanks awfully for the invitation.' But when she went to the door it was not René, but McKiley who accompanied her.

'Next time you come,' he remarked casually, 'you will take tea with me?'

'Yes. One day I'd like to.' It was a social evasion rather than acceptance on her part.

She hurried back to the house to find her patient making no secret of the fact that he had already had enough of his visitors.

'You've been a long time,' he accused unceremoniously.

'I know. I'm sorry. I've been having potato-cakes and milk with René Menden at the Dower House.' She smiled at Mrs.

72

Kimstone. 'Thank you so much for keeping Mr. Carnehill company while I was away!'

The older woman unbuttoned her lips so far as to say: 'Nonsense! We often come over and sit with him. Don't we, Roger?'

'Yes, often,' said Roger, looking as if he had only just stopped short of adding: 'Too often.'

Mrs. Kimstone made an effort and went on, with a sort of supercharged brightness: 'But, my word, you've made some changes since we were last here. All the furniture in this room—it has disappeared!'

Roger said: 'Joanna disapproved of it and turned it out. If you *must* sit on it, you'll find it in the attic,' he added pointedly.

Mrs. Kimstone ignored the invitation and asked archly: '*Who* disapproved of it?'

'I did,' put in Joanna briskly. 'As furniture it was excellent, but none of it was very suitable for a sick-room. It all had to be dusted, you know!'

Mrs. Kimstone looked slightly taken aback by this direct challenge. 'Yes, well I suppose it had. But it makes such a *bareness*—just like a hospital ward!'

'That,' murmured Roger, 'was the idea. Or so I gathered.'

Colonel Kimstone levered himself off the window-sill. 'We'd better go, Marty, and leave Roger to—to *Joanna*.' And he winked broadly.

'Are you staying to dinner?' inquired Roger, almost cordial at the prospect of release.

'We've been asked.' The Colonel gave his wife a little push towards the door. 'Have to give Mrs. Carnehill a chance to try out her latest recipes, eh Nurse?' he grinned at Joanna as they left the room.

When they had gone Joanna said, because she was beginning to be able to say such things to Roger: 'You weren't being very gracious, were you?'

'If you mean I was being a complete boor, why don't you say so?' he snapped.

'Perhaps because I've seen you behave even worse,' she said, though she was surprised at the violence of his reply.

'The woman is like a mosquito—her mind follows you around, deciding where to nip you next!'

Joanna thought she understood. 'Oh, you mean—about the furniture—?' she began laughingly.

'No, I do *not* mean about the furniture. That's nothing to the snooping she does into the more remote corners of people's private lives—' He paused, frowning. Then: 'Well, you saw René? What could he tell you?'

'Nothing. I couldn't ask him.' At risk of angering him further, she added: 'Don't you see that it would put the boy into an awkward position? It—it's too much like spying. I'd rather go straight to Mr. McKiley himself.'

'*That* would get you a long way!' put in Roger sarcastically.

'Well, as a matter of fact I did speak to him. He came in while I was at the Dower House.' She parried Roger's look of inquiry with a question of her own. 'Did you know about the timber that's being felled over by the east wall of the park?'

He frowned. 'Yes, I did.'

'Oh. Well, Mr. McKiley said that it was a good thing to do, considering the price that timber is fetching, but he didn't seem to think that you approved.' Joanna was finding this very heavy going.

'So you discussed my approval or disapproval of the disposal of my property with McKiley? I must say, Joanna, that you go rather far!'

Joanna flushed. 'I didn't know you'd been consulted about the felling. And I supposed it was one of the things you wanted to know about—'

'"A good price for it"!' fumed Roger. 'What's the good of that to me, when I don't know *what* price it fetches—when I never see an account book?'

'I put that to Mr. McKiley too,' said Joanna quietly. I suggested that you wanted and ought to have more control—'

He made a resigned gesture. 'Joanna, you're impossible. And I thought you were an ally! As if McKiley, at this stage of things, would listen to the sweet reasonableness of inviting my co-operation! But leave it—it doesn't matter.'

Joanna's heart sank. She too had begun to think of herself as an ally. And here they were, through her well-meant efforts on his behalf, at the edge of another of his despairs.

With her hand upon the bell-rope which would summon help for his bedmaking, she said slowly: 'There's one way in which you could get your way and run the estate as you please. You could determine to get well sooner than anyone expects. For instance, you could begin by trying to believe in the new treatment they are going to give you in Dublin.'

'Yes, and if I ever do get on my feet again, when all's done there'll be the Marty Kimstones of this world watching me like hawks to see what I'll do with my freedom!'

Joanna did not reply. She did not understand the implication of his last remark and it was useless to try to argue with him in such a mood.

It was Shuan who answered the summons of the bell. She was full of having gained a pupil for riding lessons and chattered away to Roger, though Joanna thought that he answered with scant interest.

'My dear,' she exclaimed, 'the woman's got a seat like a sack of potatoes and she uses her hands like a couple of flatirons. Roger, you're not listening!'

'Yes, I am. Potatoes. Flatirons. What else?'

But it seemed to Joanna that it was his eyes that followed Shuan about the room, rather than that his mind followed her chatter.

Was it possible that Mrs. Kimstone had talked about the girl, had criticized her or praised her, and now he was silently assessing the matter for himself? Before the evening was out Joanna was to know.

After dinner—which consisted of an excellent soup, grilled trout and a savoury—she was left alone with Mrs. Kimstone while the other three went off in search of confirmation of a piece of Irish history which was in dispute.

Mrs. Kimstone took from a handbag as big as a holdall a piece of shapeless grey knitting upon which her needles clicked vigorously.

'You don't knit, Nurse?' she inquired sharply.

'Sometimes. But I'm not doing anything at the moment,' admitted Joanna.

Mrs. Kimstone began to count stitches, did some calculations, frowned, and then launched herself upon some frenzied unravelling.

'I always say it's so *soothing*!' she said tritely.

'It is—when it goes well!' replied Joanna demurely, and was careful not to meet the inquiring glance of the small eyes as their owner wondered if she was being laughed at.

There was silence until the grey mass was once more dangling from the pins. Then Mrs. Kimstone said, with the same arch brightness which she had used with Roger: 'It's so nice, isn't it, to think that when Roger gets better Mrs. Carnehill's plans for her two young people will probably have a happy ending after all?'

Joanna said: 'Plans? For whom? I don't understand.'

Mrs. Kimstone tittered. 'Oh, come, Nurse! Don't pretend to be blind! Or is it that you feel, in your position here, you have to appear detached? In that case, perhaps I'd better not go on. But you mean you haven't realized what's afoot between Roger and Shuan? That Mrs. Carnehill would be so happy if they made a match between them?'

'Between *Roger* and *Shuan*?' Joanna realized too late that she had used her patient's first name aloud. 'Surely you're wrong, Mrs. Kimstone? Mrs. Carnehill, I feel certain, doesn't hope for or suspect anything of the sort!'

The tight lips pursed. 'I dare say I've known Ena Carnehill for longer than you have, Nurse! She would be delighted to have Shuan happily with Roger. After all, you can never tell with a son—the flipperty-gibbets *I've* seen imported into decent homes like

78

Carrieghmere—!'

'But Mrs. Carnehill told me that there was nothing more than a brother-and-sister relationship between them! She was quite happy about that, but—' Joanna paused, wondering why she felt so impelled to deny the possibility of an understanding between Roger and Shuan, and decided quickly that it was due to an impish desire to contradict the sharp-eyed little gossip across the hearth. She went on: 'Mrs. Carnehill did suggest that Monsieur Menden—the farm-student, you know—had begun to care for Shuan—'

'But she didn't suggest that Shuan cared for *him*?' retorted Mrs. Kimstone quickly. 'I happen to know that nothing is further from the girl's thoughts.'

'No,' said Joanna slowly, 'I don't think anyone could suppose that Shuan had any ideas in the direction of René—'

'How could she,' put in her companion triumphantly, 'when it's quite obvious that she is *devoted* to Roger?'

'But their ages!' protested Joanna. 'She is eighteen, I think. And Mr. Carnehill is—thirty? Besides, I'm with him a good deal, you know. And he has never given any indication that he—he feels in that way about Shuan.'

'*That* difference in age is of no consequence, Nurse! In fact, quite the ideal, everyone said when I married the

79

Colonel—and as for Roger's not showing his feelings, he wouldn't so much as give *me* a hint!'

'You asked him?' inquired Joanna shrewdly, suspecting that she now understood much of her patient's cryptic commentary on his visitor.

'Oh, not in so many words, of course! I probed him—very tactfully. But it's clear that he is keeping things to himself, because that's his idea of nobility—of what, in his circumstances, is the *manly* thing to do. His accident, you know!'

'His accident?'

'Yes. He feels that he ought not to "speak" while he lies there, not knowing what his future may be.'

'Then he can't be very confident of what Shuan feels for him,' said Joanna with conviction. 'And no "nobility" can justify his not telling her that he loves her if he does, of not giving her the chance to make her own decision in the matter!'

Mrs. Kimstone's eyebrows were raised distastefully. 'Dear me, Nurse, I didn't know that we were talking about *love*!'

'Then what,' cried Joanna in exasperation, 'what, in the name of goodness, *were* we talking about?'

'Surely'—the needles clicked with a kind of smug satisfaction—'we were talking of a match which everyone would find entirely suitable? I don't know that, as they've known each other since childhood, that there would be anything particularly *romantic* about it—even if that were *at all* desirable—!'

Joanna said nothing. She looked across at the self-satisfied figure opposite, upon whose dry lips the lovely words 'love' and 'romantic' had been no more than shrivelled negatives, denying all that should be most precious in life.

Mrs. Kimstone was saying rather acidly: 'You don't seem to like the idea, Nurse! Now I wonder why?'

Joanna said: 'It's not, after all, for me to like or dislike any of my patients' private plans. It's simply that I was rather surprised, in view of what Mrs. Carnehill had said to me.'

'Oh. I supposed perhaps that you might feel offended because Roger hadn't confided in you. I thought the modern nurse liked to feel that she had the *full* confidence of her patient. However, you mustn't mind if, because I've known Roger longer than you have, there are things about him that I can *sense*, without his having to tell me a teeny word!'

'I won't mind,' promised Joanna demurely, determining that though it was impossible to be annoyed with anyone so self-satisfied and obtuse, she would not say anything more upon the subject.

81

But when she reached her room that night she realized wryly that in thinking over Mrs. Kimstone's story she had achieved none of the detachment she had intended! In fact she had become quite passionate about the whole affair. She was thinking, as she put on her dressing-gown and sat down to brush her hair, that she needed something or someone to bring her back to a sense of proportion—to the realization that she was here at Carrieghmere on a case, and that deeply passionate interest in other people's private lives was certainly no part of her work.

But it was difficult to be entirely indifferent to people like those at Carrieghmere. Their unconventionalities and even their ill-humours served to make them rounded and colourful—as if, somehow, they *insisted* on your attention! It seemed that she had conveyed that even to Dale, thought Joanna with a smile. For his last letter had held an odd resentment of her preoccupation with them. If it had been anyone other than Dale she would have said he was jealous! But the letter itself was here somewhere...

After re-reading it, she sat forward, her head in her hands, while her fingers thrust deeply into the loosened falls of her hair at each side of her face. Suddenly she did not want to smile at the tone of the letter any more. Dale didn't often write like that—her own letter must have said more than she meant to convey, and Dale seemed really disturbed.

At what? What could she have said or hinted at to be taken up so seriously? She could not tell. Tomorrow she must write to him again, be really facetious this time or else ignore altogether the subject of the Carnehills and their complicated affairs.

She started at the sound of a knock upon her door. Her thoughts immediately flew to her patient—someone had come to call her, and she would have to dress and go to him.

But when the door opened it was Shuan Ferrall who stood upon the threshold. And Shuan was full of nobody's urgencies but her own.

She said breathlessly: 'Can I come in? I—I want to talk to you. I've got to get away from Carrieghmere!'

CHAPTER SIX

The two girls looked at each other for a long minute. Then Joanna said gently:

'Yes, come in. Come and sit down.'

'You were just going to bed.' It was the nearest approach to an apology for her intrusion which Shuan could be expected to attempt.

Joanna smiled. 'Getting on that way. But

I'm afraid I'm a dreadful potterer. I wasn't quite ready for bed.' She paused, then looked directly at the girl to challenge: '*Why* must you get away from home?'

'I want to. I—Oh, it's no good my staying here! But I haven't said a word to Mums. I came to you because of what you said about—about antique shops or something. You said I ought to get a job in one—'

'And *you* said it was impossible!' Joanna reminded her with a smile.

'Yes, well—I've changed my mind. I thought I'd go to Dublin.'

Joanna reflected swiftly: How careful one ought to be! On the strength of this child's smattering of knowledge about good glass *I* seem to have taken it upon myself to point her career!

Shuan went on blandly: 'Mums wouldn't let me stay there, of course. I should have to go in every day. But there's a train from Tulleen that'd get me there between ten and eleven in the morning—'

Joanna took a deep breath. This was where these vague blossomings of an artistic ambition had, regretfully, to be nipped in the bud! As gently as she could, she said:

'I don't think that would do, Shuan. You see, no establishment that was worth anything at all *to you* would want you trailing in to begin a day's work at that time. But I dare say you haven't had time to think of the practical difficulties at all. You would have to leave here very early every morning—even Saturdays!—and you'd have either to bike to Tulleen station or go in with René on the milk-float—'

'I'd bike,' put in Shuan morosely.

'Even so, you'd still have to get back the same way each evening. And what about all the things you do here? Weren't you telling Mr. Carnehill you'd got a new pupil for riding?'

'She could have her lesson on Sundays—or go without!'

'The customer,' murmured Joanna dryly, 'is always right! But then there are your dogs?'

A shadow crossed the girl's face. 'Yes, I know.' She looked truculently at Joanna. 'You suggested it,' she accused.

'I realize that. But when I did so I'm afraid I hadn't thought of the practical difficulties either. I'm sorry, Shuan. But would you care to tell me why you've suddenly decided that you want to take up the idea?'

'It's—oh, it's because of—of you and Roger!'

There was a charged silence. Then:

'What about—Mr. Carnehill and me?' asked Joanna.

'Well, since you've come he—he doesn't want me any more. I've tried to pretend to myself that he still likes me to do things for him and be with him when you're not. But it isn't any good. He's always quoting you and—well, I suddenly decided that I couldn't bear it any more! And when I told him about what you'd said about my getting a job in Dublin he said he thought it was a grand idea and why didn't I. So then I knew it wasn't any good going on trying!'

Joanna said quietly: 'This is going to be an impertinence, Shuan. Don't answer if you'd rather not. But—do you care for Mr. Carnehill *very* much?'

Beneath the deep shadow of her lashes Shuan's eyes were very bright. 'Yes— terribly,' she said.

'Then if I were you I wouldn't consider going to Dublin or anywhere else while he's ill. There are still heaps of things you can do for him. And you *waste* yourself in jealousy, Shuan. Together we could work *for* him!'

'But he doesn't *want* me any more!'

Joanna shook her head, half in exasperation, half in pity. 'He'll learn to want you less if you run away!' she declared. She felt suddenly weary, as if this struggle against the girl's convictions had drawn all virtue out of her.

Shuan was saying slowly: 'You think he does need me a bit, after all?'

'As much,' said Joanna tiredly, 'as he needs anyone outside himself. But it will be he who will cure himself in the end.'

Something of her weariness must have showed in her face, for Shuan stood up abruptly. She said: 'All right, I'll go now. And if I can do anything for Roger—anything at all!—I'll stay.' At the door she turned, said 'Thank you' with an air of its having been dragged from her, and was gone.

Afterwards Joanna sat on, resting her head in her hand and letting tiredness flow over her. She was thinking: 'So she does love him in the way I hoped, after all. It seemed to shine in her eyes when she said she cared for him. Mrs. Kimstone was wrong when she said they were taking each other for granted and that there wasn't any question of "love" between them. And I'm glad, for I wanted it to be like that for them—*didn't I?*'

★   ★   ★

The next morning Doctor Beltane telephoned to say that Roger was to go for his new treatment into a Dublin nursing home immediately.

'He'll travel by ambulance and you'll go with him, Nurse,' were his instructions. 'He'll be there for a few days and you won't be wanted during that time, of course. I dare say you'll make arrangements to get back to Carrieghmere the same evening.'

Roger himself took the news more philosophically than Joanna had hoped. Mrs.

Carnehill was frankly glad and confident, and it was Shuan, Joanna found, who needed comfort and constant reassurance that Roger would be 'all right'. She stood about, her hands thrust into the pockets of her jeans and wearing an air of would-be nonchalance. But her eyes were pathetic, and at last Roger, giving way to a flurry of irritation, was driven to expostulate.

'For pity's sake, Shuan, don't *haunt* so!' he exclaimed. 'Talk about a banshee at a wedding—!'

At that, Shuan left the room abruptly, and Joanna was shocked at the hurt behind her eyes. Poor Shuan! She was learning that the price of loving could be high.

Roger said defensively: 'Shuan wants to *give* too much!'

'It's a good fault, surely?' murmured Joanna.

'Yes, but—Well, I only know that she makes me feel more helpless than I am.'

'I daresay, when you—when you're very fond of someone it's difficult to avoid the giving process,' said Joanna slowly.

'I suppose so. But Shuan and I should understand each other better by now. She should know that there are things she can't give me or share with me. She can't do my living for me—I wouldn't ask that she should try.'

As Joanna answered him quietly:

'That still doesn't prevent her wanting to "do your living for you", as you call it,' she wanted to cry to him instead:

'Don't you see that if a woman loves enough she *must* want to give all that and more? That in love there's no such thing as "giving too much"? You must give all you have and still feel shamed by the utter poverty of it? Don't you *see*—?'

She came back to reality to realize that Roger was regarding her shrewdly.

He said: 'A man has got to work out his own destiny. No one—least of all a woman—can do it for him. Tell me, Joanna, did you ever make the mistake of trying?'

'I don't know. Perhaps I've wanted to.'

Roger's eyebrows went up and his mouth lifted in a half-smile. 'How unwise of you!' he mocked. 'And who was the victim? The young man in London—Dale somebody—the apothecary chap?'

Joanna laughed, accepting gratefully his lighter mood. 'No—and he isn't that kind of a chemist!'

'Well, perhaps it was an earlier flame of yours—or a later?'

'It was neither. It was for someone I didn't know very well at the time. So that only made it a double impertinence, didn't it?'

He looked at her seriously again now. 'I don't know,' he said slowly. 'I've got a feeling that a man might accept a lot from you,

89

Joanna. You would give—but you'd never thrust. Once—a little while ago—I asked you to help me. I'd never heard myself doing that to anyone else!'

Joanna said: 'But why shouldn't you? It's what I'm here for.' And could not tell him that it was his own destiny she had longed to influence—his and Shuan's—when she had willed last night that they at least should know the heights and the depths and all the sharp realities of the thing called love.

The nursing home to which Roger was taken was just off St. Stephen's Green in the heart of the city, and when Joanna had left him there she walked out into the tree-lined square, meaning to find her way down to Grafton Street and O'Connell Street of which she had heard so much, before taking a train for her return to Carrieghmere.

But as she was crossing the road, being absorbed in the sights about her, there was a sudden scream of car-brakes, and Justin McKiley's luxurious car pulled in to the curb as she reached it.

He said without ceremony: 'Do you usually treat buses in that high-handed fashion?'

Joanna laughed. 'Oh, I'm sorry! *And* for getting in your way if you wanted to pass the bus—'

'I didn't,' said McKiley easily. 'I was making for the Shelbourne to get a drink. What about lunching with me there?'

90

Joanna hesitated. 'I was going back to Carrieghmere early this afternoon,' she said.

He brushed aside the objection. 'Ah, what's the hurry? You came in with Roger, didn't you? Well then, lunch with me; I'll give you a glimpse of the city afterwards, and you'll drive down to Carrieghmere with me later on. How's that?'

'I must phone Mrs. Carnehill,' said Joanna firmly. 'She'll want to hear how Mr. Carnehill stood the journey.'

'Well, you can do that from the Shelbourne. It's just here.'

Joanna gave in, and presently they were seated opposite to each other in the dining-room of the hotel. After lunch they drove in a leisurely way about the city while Justin pointed out things of interest.

Then in the late afternoon the nose of the car was turned to the south-west and the flat white ribbon of road which would take them back to Carrieghmere.

Joanna was content not to talk but to watch the unfamiliar countryside. However, after a long silence her companion said suddenly:

'Well, how do you like the job now?'

'As much as I expected,' was Joanna's even reply.

He laughed. 'H'm. Not giving away much, are you? You mean you find the young man's moods and caprices—bearable?'

'Do you mind,' asked Joanna quietly, 'if we

don't discuss my patient—?'

'Sorry.' His tone was amused, indifferent. 'But may I remind you that at the Dower House the other day *you* began a discussion of him with *me*!'

'Yes. That was different. It wasn't personal.'

'Neither was this meant to be personal with regard to him. It was personal—about you.'

'Well, will you take it that I find my case a very satisfactory one and that I'm not involved personally at all?'

'Not at all? Do you know, I find that difficult to believe. Frequently tiresome as I find Roger myself, he has some appeal to the female of the species, surely?'

'I don't know. I never thought about it. I'm merely his nurse.'

Justin shrugged his shoulders. 'And you're not discussing your patient? All right. This is where we came in—Now what about a gesture of friendliness in place of the frozen mitt? Come along to the Dower House to an impromptu party of mine this evening?'

'I'm in uniform. Should I have time to change?'

'Of course. I've got some people coming out from Dublin, but they won't be there before seven, and we shall be back long before that. Will you come?'

Joanna had thought already of the anti-climax of the return to Carrieghmere to dine with Mrs. Carnehill and a morose Shuan and to have no particular duties of her own until Roger's return.

So she said: 'I must see Mrs. Carnehill first. But if she can spare me for a little while—yes, I'll come.'

'You will, so? Good. Then I'll expect you.'

As she was changing, later on, Joanna realized that this would be her first social occasion since she had come to Eire. She remembered her early shock at sight of Tulleen and how she had wondered how one 'stepped out'—if one wanted to. Oddly enough, since coming to Carrieghmere she had not seemed to have time to miss cinemas, shops or people.

When she reached the Dower House she found that there were several cars drawn up outside it, and the room which had been closed when she had previously gone there was already more than half full of people.

The room itself seemed to express Justin McKiley well enough. The furnishings were ultra-modern, from the fluorescent lighting of the off-white carpet, from the oddly angled chairs to the black glass panels which formed a large part of the wall surface.

Joanna thought with amusement: 'A far cry, this from the castor-oil plant and the bamboo across the hall!'

Justin McKiley came over, apologized for not having seen her as soon as she arrived.

Then his sweeping glance surveyed her from the shining gold of her hair to her nylon-clad ankles. He said:

'You wear uniform like a devotee. But you wear clothes like—a woman!'

The words were a compliment, but the look and tone which accompanied them were an enigma. Joanna flushed, wondering how it had come about that the man supposed he could say such things to her. But without waiting for a reply he took her informally by the wrist and drew her among the other guests in order to introduce her.

The introductions were of the usual kind at such parties—the unheard names, the exchange of a few polite words, and the relieved return to intimate, allusive conversation as soon as the newcomer had been taken on to the next group. Joanna had begun to hope she would meet someone to whom she wanted to talk or who would want to talk to her. She was glad when René Menden stepped forward to claim her attention and after a moment's hesitation McKiley left her to him and to his companion, an auburn-haired girl dressed in white. She too glanced appraisingly at Joanna from beneath the astonishingly long lashes which shaded her dark, almond-shaped eyes. In a quick glance of her own Joanna saw that all the accessories to her white gown were black—she wore black ear-rings, was smoking a cigarette in a black holder, and carried an enormous black handbag. She had an air of extreme sophistication and Joanna's single brief thought before the other girl spoke was: 'How well she fits in with—all this!'

'My name is Magda.' The lazy voice that matched the lazy almond eyes made its own introduction before René had time to speak. 'What's yours?'

'Joanna. Joanna Merivale.' She paused, hoping that the girl named Magda would see fit to add her own surname. But she said only: 'Oh. Joanna is enough. I should never remember the Merivale part, anyway.' She turned to René. 'I don't know that I've ever even heard yours?'

René smiled. 'It does not matter. You would not remember it either.'

Magda blew a smoke-ring in his direction. 'He's sweet, isn't he?' she inquired of Joanna.

Joanna did not reply, thinking how inapt the adjective was for describing René, who was intelligent and well mannered and certainly nothing so inadequate as 'sweet'.

While they talked she noticed that frequently only half of the other girl's attention seemed to be with her companions; the other part was with her eyes which, veiled though they were, followed Justin McKiley everywhere he moved about the room. But when at last he came across to rejoin them she half-turned her back upon him, feigning an indifference which Joanna was sure she did not feel.

She said carelessly over her shoulder: 'A *lovely* party, Justin. *All* the old familiar faces! Don't you ever invite anyone new?'

Again he took Joanna's wrist lightly between his finger and thumb. 'You're meeting Joanna,' he said. 'She's new!'

'I mean men, of course!' she retorted, and Joanna was startled at the look of contempt which crossed her face.

Justin dropped Joanna's wrist and leaned towards the other girl as he took a light from her cigarette. He said intently: 'But Magda does not need new men—or does she?'

'Every woman,' put in René sententiously, 'needs new men! For the development of her character it is of the most essential!'

Justin ignored the interruption as he repeated, his eyes still holding Magda's own: '*Or does she?*'

She shrugged. 'One gets bored,' she said. 'Especially when it is obvious that your parties are business affairs as much as social. Lately you don't invite anyone who isn't likely to be of use to you—'

A look, the meaning of which Joanna did not understand, passed between them then. But when Justin spoke again his tone was as light and mocking as ever. He said: 'Come, that's unjust of you! Not even you, Magda dear, could suggest that Joanna here is merely utilitarian! Of the most decorative, surely?' His mimicry was very sure, and René took in good part the laughter against himself, in which, however, Magda did not share.

Justin contemplated the dark storminess of her face for a minute or two. Then he turned deliberately to Joanna. 'On the contrary, it is you who must be getting bored!' he said easily. 'May I find you someone else to talk to?'

The rebuff to Magda was patent, and Joanna felt embarrassed for her. But her manner asked no one's pity, least of all Joanna's, as she was stung to action by the snub.

She made an imperious gesture to René and with his help shrugged her shoulders into a wide-panniered coat. You too,' she said pointedly to him, 'must find someone else to talk to, for I am leaving now!'

Justin made a sudden movement towards her. 'Surely not?' he asked. 'I meant to drive you back myself.'

She glanced at him, her eyelashes fluttering lazily. 'Thanks,' she drawled. 'But I came with the Salmonds and they'll take me back. How could I drag you away from the novelty of which you seem so proud?' This time her glance included Joanna and her meaning was plain.

She moved across the room to speak to a

man and woman in another group, waited for them as they came over to Justin McKiley in order to take their leave, and presently left with them.

Justin looked down at Joanna and said reflectively: 'There was a time when I once thought Magda was unique. Now I'm inclined to believe that she's merely—human!'

He was offering Joanna another drink now, but she indicated the glass of sherry which René had brought to her and which she had not yet finished. Then he said, watching René as he moved away:

'I suppose I should have invited Shuan for him. But she treats him so abominably that it doesn't make things easier for him—harder, in fact. So that makes it a kindness to René to keep them apart.'

Joanna said slowly: 'She is very transparent. She finds it difficult to conceal anything that she feels—'

'—And I dare say hasn't made any secret of the fact that she regards *you* as an interloper?' Again his glance appraised her. 'You know, I must admit that she has some justification for jealousy.'

'That's absurd!' retorted Joanna hotly.

'Is it? Do you still claim that that uniform of yours will shelter you from *everything*? What about Magda, for instance? Didn't *her* reaction to you teach you anything at all?'

'Magda—I'm afraid she didn't tell me her other name—struck me as being rather bored with her surroundings and without any interest whatsoever in me,' said Joanna calmly. 'Whatever resentment she showed was because you—you *flaunted* me at her. But that she was *jealous* of me as you suggest Shuan might be—that's absurd!'

'*Is* it?' asked Justin McKiley again. 'I wonder!'

CHAPTER SEVEN

When Roger was brought back from Dublin he looked white and shaken from the rigors of the 'new treatment' which he had undergone.

Mrs. Carnehill hovered at his bedside, her longing to suffer for him written in every line of her face.

'You're in pain, Roger—!'

He managed a rueful smile for her. 'No, that's the devil of it. At least, though the top half of me is harried and wracked by every ache that was ever invented, none of it's in the right places. In my back, where I'm assured I ought to feel something, there's nothing—nothing at all. But Carnehills always were contrary, weren't they?'

'But the feeling will come back, Roger. It must!' The conviction in her voice was buoyed by hope alone.

'It will. About by the time the humidity of our darling climate has me twisted into a gnarled knot with arthritis in my seventies! Wasn't I reading somewhere that certain ailments take immediate hook at the mere suggestion of old man arthritis—or was it the other way about—he hops it at sight of them? Joanna, do you know?'

Joanna turned about from the table where she had been measuring his medicine. Her lip twitched as she said gravely:

'I believe in America they've discovered that arthritis doesn't live alongside yellow jaundice, pregnancy or starvation. If you think you're likely to qualify, I hope you'll let me know.'

He laughed, and Mrs. Carnehill joined in before she left the room. But when she had gone his face darkened again, and he said morosely: 'Mother destroys herself with worry about me. I wish she wouldn't. What good does it do? And, as soon as she gets back from Naas, it'll be Shuan next. "*Darling* Roger—" No, Joanna, I can't stand much more. You must keep her away, or make her pipe down or something—'

'They—they care too much,' Joanna said slowly. 'It's understandable. And you don't always bear with them as you might. Just now you were cleverer—you made Mrs. Carnehill laugh. You might try that more often.'

100

'But why must they get so—so emotional about it? Why can't they accept the dreary inevitability of it all and not let themselves get so worked up? *You* don't!'

'For me it's rather different, isn't it?'

'It is? Yes, I suppose it is. You know, I thought about you a lot while I was in the nursing home—'

'Did you?' Even to Joanna her voice sounded as if it came from a long way off.

'Yes. Don't appear too interested, will you? Though I admit I'd have been tempted to have you strangled if you'd said: "Flattered, I'm sure," or "Did you? How nice!" Anyway, don't you want to know at *all* what I thought?'

'Yes, go on—'

'Well, I had fiendish nights, mostly, and I spent most of 'em thinking. And I remembered an odd thing that Denis Johnston once said—he's one of our dramatists, by the way. He said that none of us was convinced of the *reality* of anybody but ourselves. Anyway, I began to check up on the people who were real to *me* . . . Mother is, of course, and Shuan and McKiley, blast him . . . René only vaguely, I'm afraid. And that brought me to you. I thought: "Joanna?" And do you know, I found that you were— utterly real?'

'You were surprised at that?'

'Yes, I think I was. I should have expected

101

length of time of knowing a person could count a lot. And how long have you been at Carrieghmere? A few weeks, isn't it? And then you're so correct and impersonal about the job—and you haven't talked much about yourself. In fact you've got all the qualification for being a mere frontage. But you're not, though of course I realize that, *to you*, I'm no more than a symbol in your case-book. Do nurses keep case-books?'

Joanna smiled. 'Only officially.'

'But I am no more than that?' he persisted.

She hesitated. Then she said slowly: 'No. You are "real" too.'

'You'd have to say that, lest I think you completely case-hardened and soulless!'

'No, it's true. I've realized for some time that all of Carrieghmere and all the people in it and about it have as much reality for me as any place or almost any people I have ever known. It's as—as if it were a place I'd had a nostalgia, a sort of homesickness for, all my life.' She laughed diffidently. 'That's impossible, of course. How could I be homesick for a place I'd never seen?'

Roger commented: 'It's improbable, rather. You've lived in London all your life. You must hanker for everything it offers. Be honest, Joanna. One day you'll turn a thankful back upon the rains and the loneliness and the interminable bog. Before long Carrieghmere and all it stands for will be part of your past.' He took the medicine glass from her and regarded her quizzically over the rim of it. 'Do you know, I resent uncommonly the thought of being relegated to anyone's past!'

Joanna looked at her watch for, lightly questioning though his glance was, her own eyes did not want to meet it. She said briskly: 'Well, you're very much of my immediate present now. In fact, all of us revolve about you—you should be thankful for that!'

*　　　*　　　*

It was about a week later. She was in the kitchen, preparing a tray for her patient, and Mrs. Carnehill was there too, knitting her brows over the adaptation of a Portuguese fish delicacy.

They both looked up as the sound of heavy footsteps sounded in the yard outside, and Michael, the stable-lad of whom Dr. Beltane had said his heart 'was in mechanics', came rather diffidently into the kitchen.

He blushed at sight of Joanna and said to Mrs. Carnehill: 'Could I be sayin' a word to ye, ma'am?'

Mrs. Carnehill regarded him vaguely. 'Yes, Michael. What is it you want?'

'Well, ma'am—' He stopped and shook his head. 'No. 'Tis the terrible liberty, after all—'

Mrs. Carnehill laid down a tablespoon and withdrew the pencil from behind her ear with an air of abandoning everything she was doing until Michael had got his message off his chest.

'Look, Michael,' she said patiently, 'we have all this modest blarney from you whenever you have a favour to ask. What is it this time?'

'Well, ma'am—would ye be wantin' the car at all tomorrow?'

'No. Why? But wait now—I would. I have to go to Belfast, and Shuan must drive me into Tullen.'

Michael, whose face had dropped, looked more hopeful. 'Tulleen, is it? 'Tis but the lick of a journey at all. The car'd be free after that, supposing—supposing anyone wanted to borrow it?'

'It would—supposing *you* wanted to borrow it! And what would you want with it, you spalpeen?'

'To take it to Dublin. To—to take Roseen to Dublin. For hasn't she her heart set on one o' thim husky film stars and will give me no peace till she has me at the Rialto to see him cavortin' on the screen? 'Tis a small thing, she says, to ask Mrs. Carnehill could you have the car one day, the way it'd be sittin' on its four wheels the while nobody would be needin' it at all. But, of course 'tis not a small thing, as I told her—'

Mrs. Carnehill's eyes twinkled. 'Go on with you, Michael! You know you thought of it yourself!'

'I did not, so!'

'Well, it's all one. Yes, you can have it when Shuan brings it back from Tulleen. But no acrobatics, mind! And no staying till the last house.'

The boy grinned his thanks and had turned away when Mrs. Carnehill reached for her handbag and produced a crumpled treasury note from it.

'Here, you wretch,' she said as she thrust it into his hand. 'Give Roseen a good time and see that she realizes that film stars aren't for the likes of her nor for any of us!'

When he had gone she chuckled. 'Roseen'll take him in the end,' she told Joanna confidently.

'Oh, are they—?'

'—like that? Yes, I think so. Though Roseen declares she has her heart set on going for a nurse, and you'd often say that the Kilkenny cats were nothing to the pair of them! But she has admitted to me that Michael has "char-r-m"; I've no doubt the loan of the car will put it high indeed!'

★   ★   ★

The next day Mrs. Carnehill, in the usual flurry which accompanied the preparations for her journeys, set off for several days in Belfast, and when Shuan brought back the car Roseen, in a sky-blue dress and camel-hair coat, and Michael, almost unrecognizable in a bow-tie, left upon their own jaunt. And Joanna happened to be crossing the hall when the telegram came...

'For Merivale,' said the impersonal voice at the other end of the wire.

'Merivale here,' said Joanna.

'Handed in in London. The message says: "Arriving Dublin unexpectedly seventeenth. Very brief stay Trinity College to watch important experiment. Must see you. Shall expect you T.C. any time during afternoon. Looking forward so much. Signed—Dale." Do you want a confirmation?'

'No—no, it doesn't matter.' Joanna replaced the receiver, wanting nothing so much as a little time now in which to digest the telegram's contents. Dale in Dublin! And this was the seventeenth itself. He must have flown over and be already there.

Her first impulse was to say that she could not possibly go—to ring up Trinity College in the hope of finding him and saying that she could not possibly get to Dublin at such short notice. For somehow—for a vague reason which she could not define—she felt that *personally* she needed longer notice before leaving to meet Dale again.

She was shocked at that. Was it possible

that in no more than a few weeks at Carrieghmere she had travelled so far from the routine of her life in London that she wanted warning of seeing Dale whom, there, she saw at least once or twice a week?

It was no more than vanity, she told herself ... Instinctively, on taking the telegram she had made that mental feminine review. 'What can I put on? I wish I'd washed my hair—' But she knew in her heart that her reluctance went deeper. A meeting with Dale would call for adjustments...

She was still standing irresolutely by the telephone when Shuan came into the hall. She stared at Joanna, whose hand still rested upon the receiver, and asked abruptly:

'Is anything wrong? Have you had bad news?'

Joanna pulled herself together with a jerk. 'No. Only rather unexpected news. A—a friend of mine is in Dublin for a day or two, and he wired before leaving England to see if I could meet him there. It was all rather sudden. Probably that's why I was looking a bit lost!'

'Well, are you going?'

'No. How can I? He wants to see me today and I can't get even to Tulleen to catch a train. Besides, I oughtn't to leave you alone with Mr. Carnehill.'

'You mean you don't intend to!' A dark flush mounted in the girl's face as she went on passionately. 'There's utterly no reason why you shouldn't leave him to me for a day. But you don't mean to, even though you could do it quite easily. You could have Patrick Sheehan's taxi from Tulleen or, better still, you could go into Dublin with Justin. I've just met him, and he offered me a lift if I wanted to go, so why shouldn't he take you?'

Joanna took a sudden resolution. She said quietly: 'Shuan, you know that since we talked that night I've tried to let you help Mr. Carnehill in every way I could think of. And because I believe he will be all right with you I've decided to go to Dublin, if Mr. McKiley will take me.'

Shuan's face cleared as quickly as it had clouded. 'You *know* he'll be all right with me. Are you going to tell him?'

'Yes, of course.'

'Well, I'll go and tell Justin to wait for you. I'll say that he must bring you back too.'

Roger's acceptance of Joanna's news was one of gloomy resignation. But before she left him to go to change he said: 'When we were talking about the people who were our "realities" I said I should resent being relegated to your past. Now I find I don't want to believe that you've got a present which isn't wholly concerned with me and your life here. But the young man—the apothecary, I suppose he is one of your "realities"?'

'Yes,' said Joanna firmly, 'he is. I've known him far too long for him to be anything else.' At the door she paused, looked back over her shoulder, and said with a twinkle: 'But he still isn't an apothecary.'

Before she closed the door behind her she had the gratification of hearing Roger chuckle.

★   ★   ★

As she changed out of her uniform she found her mood altering. She did want to go to Dublin to see Dale after all! And she gave a good deal of care—though she had not much time—to what she would wear.

When finally she ran downstairs to Justin McKiley's waiting car she had chosen a full-skirted black coat with a dress of grey jersey under it. Her matching hat of jersey was half beret, half bonnet, and she carried a handbag of grey lizard which had cost far too much, and over which she had many purse-searchings before she had decided to afford it.

Justin McKiley looked at her with frank admiration, but he made no remark upon her appearance until she told him how grateful she was for the lift. Then he said meaningly: 'The person who should really be grateful to me is the fortunate man for whose sake I'm taking you to Dublin at all!'

It was an open invitation to tell him more about her errand, and Joanna felt she could do no less than do so.

He made no comment, but said casually: 'Shuan asked me to bring you back again this evening. Is that right?'

'If you are able—?'

'Well, I'm giving Magda—you remember Magda?—a drink at the Greville at about half-seven. Could you come there?'

Joanna did not know where the Greville was, but he told her, and though she was not anxious to meet Magda again she promised to meet him there.

Before long, the car was sliding into the neat suburbs of the city and Justin asking where he should leave her. She asked to be set down on O'Connell Bridge, and when she had watched the car go on up O'Connell Street she crossed over to Trinity College and inquired with some trepidation at the porter's lodge for Dale. It was all wrong to be feeling so—so *apart* from him in so short a time!

She was asked to wait in a waiting-room and there, presently, he came to her.

'Joanna!' Both his hands came out to take hers. 'So you got my wire?'

'Yes. What—what a surprise, Dale!' She sounded a little breathless.

'It was. But you may imagine that I jumped at the chance to come over.'

'How long is it for?'

110

'Three days. 'I've got to be present at two experiments and a lecture tomorrow. But today I'm free. That's why I was able to give you so little notice. What shall we do? What is the city like?'

They walked out side by side into the pale sunshine, and Joanna knew that she was thinking: 'I wish he would say that I look nice or—or even well.' But she remembered that Dale rarely said anything like that. Which was comforting when you knew you weren't looking your best, but was rather dampening when you hoped that you were.

As they walked up O'Connell Street he asked again. 'Well, what are we going to do? Is there anywhere we could go to talk? What do you do yourself when you come here?'

'I don't,' said Joanna quickly. 'I've been only once before, when I had to bring Mr. Carnehill to the nursing home for treatment. But if you want to see sights, there's the Hill of Howth up there'—she waved a hand vaguely northwards—'or there's Killiney down there. You climb them and get a magnificent view, I gather—'

'I said,' repeated Dale patiently, 'that I wanted to talk, not look at views, however magnificent.' For the first time he seemed really to look at her. 'Besides, you're in your best bib and tucker. You're not dressed for climbing things.'

Subtly—and most unreasonably—Joanna

111

felt irritated. The reluctant sunshine was warm now; she felt stifled by the city and would have welcomed a tramp at Dale's side, reliving the many times when they had walked over Box Hill or Berkhamsted Common together. Her clothes *weren't* unsuitable for it! And he had no right to imply that she had only one 'party best' to her name!

But he was asking: 'How long shall we have together, Joanna? When must you be back?'

She told him then about Justin McKiley's having brought her and that she must be at the Greville at half-past seven at latest.

'Then we shan't have time for much more than tea,' said Dale sensibly. And, feeling ashamed of her irritation, she agreed that they wouldn't.

They found an underground café of 'Ye Bog Oak' type and as she followed Dale's familiar back down the stairs she thought: 'It's best like this. This is where we belong.' For in London they had talked across the tables of a score of such cafés. They would talk here, and she would be rid of this feeling of 'apartness' from him which nothing had served to dispel.

Downstairs, the lantern-lit atmosphere was as warm as that of a sheltered cave. Dale took off his overcoat, passed his hands over his hair, and looked approvingly at the deserted tables.

'We can talk here,' he said. 'Might be in our own home.'

He began to tell her of the experiments he had come to Dublin to see, of his own recent work, of a new assistant in the laboratory—a girl who was 'a fool but fairly easy on the eye'—and all the gossip he had been able to cull from her own headquarters, the Marrone Nursing Home.

Suddenly he looked at her more closely. 'There's an idea going around among your old cronies that you're overworked. You don't appear to have written much to anyone. Now I come to think of it, you do look tired.'

Joanna refilled his cup. 'It's the lighting,' she said more shortly than she intended.

'It's not. I noticed it outside. It's what I said in one of my letters—you're taking the whole thing too seriously, you're exhausting yourself over these people. I've never known you to do it before when you were on a case. And the chap sounds such a curmudgeon. That alone must be nervously exhausting.'

'He's frequently a curmudgeon because he probably knows more about nervous exhaustion than I hope I ever shall,' Joanna pointed out.

Dale fingered the edge of a plate. 'Yes, but—well, it's your *personal* preoccupation with it all that worries me. In the course of no more than a few weeks you seem to be intent on wrapping yourself around their lives!'

'You can't live in close contact with people like the Carnehills without finding even their oddnesses—absorbing,' commented Joanna dryly. 'I'm sorry I wrote so fully about them if you weren't interested. Of course, I couldn't expect you to be—'

'Well, they all sound mad. And you're not even interested in me any more. I've watched you while I've been talking. And you've scarcely been listening!'

Joanna laid a hand lightly over his. 'Don't be silly, Dale. Of course I've been listening. It was just what I wanted—to hear you talk and to—to realize how well I know you after all!'

It was the wrong thing to say, and he fastened upon it.

'So you *have* been moving away from me during these weeks? I sensed it somehow.'

'Simply travelling alone, I think,' answered Joanna thoughtfully. 'I haven't had much time to myself, and yet I've been extraordinarily—alone.'

Dale took that literally. He said in reply. 'Well, of course you haven't been away so far to a case before. And it's been longer than most, hasn't it?'

Joanna was conscious of an acute disappointment. How could she make him understand that it was a different kind of loneliness she had wanted to express—a loneliness of the heart, a reaching-out, a hungering for something as yet beyond her dreams?

She could not try.

So she answered him in his own mood. She said: 'Mrs. Craigie's case was much longer.'

'Yes, but you were only in Surrey. I'd like to be in a position to tell your matron to send a relief, to bring you back to Town for a bit, even if you came out again later. *I'm* missing you! Don't you realize that?'

He looked so injured that Joanna had to smile. She reached for her gloves as she said lightly: 'Well, I'm glad you're not in any such position. This is my case and I want to stay on it to the end. It—it challenges me!'

They regained the street to find that they had sat longer over tea than they realized. It was almost time for Joanna to go to the Greville to meet Justin McKiley. Like their tea-shop, the lounge of the Greville was artificially darkened rather than lighted, by means of heavy oak beaming and antique lanterns hung around the walls. They were forced to accustom their eyes to the dimness before Joanna was able to distinguish Justin McKiley talking to the girl named Magda in a corner.

Magda was in blue this evening—a sharp 'electric' blue which most women could not wear at night at all. But it suited her vivid looks to perfection. She was looking less bored than at Justin's party and was talking animatedly to him as the other two threaded their way towards them.

It was she who saw and recognized Joanna first. Instantly her heavy lids veiled her eyes. But her lips still wore a smile as she said to her companion:

'Why, here comes your "novelty"! This is a surprise. You didn't tell me that there was to be a rendezvous!'

Justin McKiley swung about, setting his glass down on the table behind him. He smiled a greeting to Joanna, glanced briefly and appraisingly at Dale, and over his shoulder answered Magda:

'Perhaps I didn't mean you to know!'

It was a deliberate, provocative taunt and, though between intimate friends it could have been taken lightly, the swift frown which crossed Magda's smooth brow showed that she had not taken it so.

Nor indeed had Dale, as Joanna could sense from the slight stiffening of his figure at her side. She glanced up at him and he down at her, his lips set in a thin line.

She felt more than angry with McKiley. By that one remark he had deliberately hinted at some relationship which did not exist between them. And Dale actually believed in it!

CHAPTER EIGHT

Three-quarters of an hour later she was sitting in silence at Justin McKiley's side as he guided the car through the suburban streets.

She was thinking of the brief foursome, the cordiality of which had had no real chance from the moment of that ill-timed joke of his.

Before they parted Dale had taken her aside to say:

'I shall be free again the day after tomorrow, Joanna. You'll come in again?'

She had said: 'I'll try, Dale, I mustn't promise. It depends how things are at Carrieghmere—'

His mouth had hardened again and he did not smile as he replied significantly:

'Of *course* it depends how things are at Carrieghmere! I'm beginning to understand that. But you should come. I think we ought to talk to each other.'

'But it was only a joke! Only to tease Magda.'

'Or to intrigue me? To set me wondering just what the standing between you is? I'm thinking that I've been inclined to underestimate the opposition at Carrieghmere. McKiley is a woman's man. You realize that, don't you? I wish you'd described him more fully—given me an idea of the sort of fellow I was going to meet. *Why* didn't you?'

'I don't know. Somehow he didn't signify.'

'Didn't he?' Dale caught at the phrase gratefully. 'I'm glad about that. Joanna, you will come in to Dublin again before I go back to England?'

Now Justin, apparently unconscious of the rift he had done his best to cause, was merely amused at Magda's latest display of ill-humour.

When he began to talk of it Joanna said quietly:

'It seemed to me that you did your best to provoke it.'

'Well'—he paused to swing the car round a corner—'Magda enjoys intriguing me. There's no reason why I shouldn't play the same game upon occasion.'

'You involved *me*,' Joanna pointed out.

'Come! You enjoyed it! Any woman likes to be played off against another. Besides, Magda happens to enjoy fighting, so I take care to provide her with a test every now and again. She would despise me for being dull if I didn't.'

He went on easily: 'Of course, I can't afford to quarrel with Magda. She has—contacts that are too valuable to me. Tell me now, have you ever realized the extent to which a clever woman can be of value to a man?'

She said lightly: 'I've always heard that a clever wife can be of inestimable value!'

'A wife. Yes.' He pondered this, then gave a laugh that was slightly out of control. 'And yet—Magda as a wife? No, that doesn't fit!'

Silence fell for a minute or two. Then, in order to change the subject Joanna remarked upon the performance of the car.

He accepted the compliment without comment. Then, leaning forward over the wheel as if to peer into the darkness ahead, he said dryly: 'You're wanting to ask, of course, how, on the pay of an agent, I manage to run a car like this at all!'

Joanna was beginning: 'I'm not very interested—' when there was a sudden checking upon the smooth movement of the car and her companion uttered an exclamation. There was another jerk and his foot thrust down upon the accelerator; another check, and he was forced to pull up.

Joanna's heart sank. 'What's the matter?' she inquired.

'A bit of a choke, maybe. Or no—' he indicated the petrol-gauge. 'Empty, I'm afraid.'

'You mean—you can't get us to Carrieghmere?' Joanna was too worried to take the check philosophically. If there were any length of delay here she would be very late back at Carrieghmere, and Shuan was alone with Roger. She wanted to gasp with impatience. This, she supposed, was where the Irish temperament could say: 'Ach, there's time enough'—and mean it. But she could not.

'Well, what do we do?' she demanded.

Justin stretched his legs comfortably before him. 'Having reviewed the situation, presumably we accept our fate,' he said maddeningly.

'But—but I can't! I must get back to Carrieghmere. Shuan has been left alone long enough.'

'Well, do you propose to get out and push? After all, no one could suggest that the delay is your fault.'

'But there must be something we can do. We can't just *sit* here!'

'Why not? Besides, we're not just sitting. I, at least, am reviewing the situation—'

She knew by the light unconcern in his voice that he appreciated nothing of the seriousness of their plight as she saw it. '*Please*,' she said. 'There must be something we can do!'

Lazily he put up a hand and switched on the interior light above their heads. By its adequate glow he looked at her.

'Say "please" again—just as you said it then,' he demanded. 'It actually achieved the effect of making you appear—vulnerable!'

She ignored the remark and did her best to

conceal her instinctive movement of recoil. She laid a hand upon the door-handle.

'Well,' she said lightly, 'since I'm the one who is anxious to be upon her way, I could always walk. How far is it to Carrieghmere?'

He laughed. 'Another fifteen miles.'

'Fifteen miles? So far?' Her dismay sounded in her voice.

'Thereabouts. Do you still mean to walk?'

'No, of course not. But hasn't your own "review of the situation" yielded anything yet?'

'Nothing. Except that rescue will ultimately be achieved. Until then I am content. I am sheltered from the elements, I have a lovely, if hitherto unapproachable, companion—'

Joanna's patience snapped. Conciliation, she decided, was useless. She riposted quickly: 'And you're behaving like the villain of a melodrama! Do try to realize that this could—could cost me my job.'

If she had sought to impress him she had failed. He said merely 'Job? When I could offer you a more attractive one at three times the money?'

'I'm not interested,' she retorted distantly. 'Merely, for the moment, in getting back to my present one. What do you propose to do about it?'

'Nothing, I think. Nothing, that is, without encouragement which you could give—'

He bent over her, his intention plain. He was saying urgently: 'We could make a team, you and I. "A clever woman"—Magda is that. But you could be more—'

Joanna shrank farther into the corner of her seat. This was the sort of 'cheap' situation for which, hitherto, she would always have said a woman had only herself to blame. She did not know what kind of co-operation with him Justin McKiley was hinting at. She only knew that she did not want to share it or anything else with him, and that Carrieghmere, a long fifteen miles away, was a kindly refuge which she could not reach without his help.

She began a little unsteadily: 'This is absurd—' but broke off as the distant sound of a car was to be heard upon the flat bog-road.

Justin heard it too: he sat back in his own seat, took a cigarette and said with a shrug: 'Sir Galahad approaches! That's what you're thinking?'

'Merely,' retorted Joanna crisply, 'that it's a car, that it's going our way, and that it can probably do something for us.' She was out on the road by this time, ready to step into the beam of the approaching headlights. But now he was at her side, drawing her back and preparing to flag the oncoming car himself.

'At least,' he said lazily, 'you might let me *play* the gentleman!'

Joanna was too anxious to reply, and waited in silence until she saw with relief that the car was slowing. Then she gave a start of recognition. Of course! Why hadn't she thought of it! It was the Carrieghmere car itself—its occupants were Michael and Roseen, themselves returning from Dublin.

Michael alighted and came forward. ''Tis Mr. McKiley, surely?'

'It is,' came the dry reply. 'Have you got any spare petrol aboard?'

'Bless me soul, I have not! Are ye dry, now? Will I nip back to Arneen or the next place beyond, to see could I get ye some in a can?'

But at this Joanna stepped forward. Michael's 'nipping back' to anywhere along the road would mean she would be forced to another session alone with Justin McKiley. And that she did not want. She said quite firmly:

'I can't help feeling that the important thing is to get me back to Carrieghmere. So if Mr. McKiley wouldn't mind the delay I think it would be better if I came along with you and Roseen, and then you could bring petrol back afterwards from there. Do you mind—?'

Her brief appeal to her companion was perfunctory, formal, and he was wise enough to recognize it as such. He made a gesture towards a bow in her direction as he said equally formally: 'The urgency is yours

123

entirely—' and strolled back nonchalantly towards his own car. When they started, for a long way down the road the beam from its powerful headlights seemed to pursue them. Then, at a dip, it winked and disappeared.

★　　　★　　　★

At Carrieghmere at last, Roseen uttered a single 'Good night' to them both and scuttled away in the direction of the kitchen regions. Joanna alighted and was asking Michael if he could go back to Justin's car with petrol when the house door flew open abruptly and Shuan, a wildly dishevelled figure, was silhouetted against the light behind her.

She almost hurled herself at Joanna as she half-sobbed: 'Oh, thank goodness you've come. Thank goodness you've come! Roger has been in terrible pain for an hour or more. I haven't been able to get Beltie and I haven't known *what* to do. Thank *goodness* you've come at last!'

Joanna's heart, which had seemed to turn over sickeningly, quieted and steadied. Even the shock of realization that she had unwittingly left the girl to deal with the utterly unlooked-for onset of crisis was submerged beneath the urgent necessity to check her rising hysteria, to act for the best swiftly, at once.

Over her shoulder she spoke sharply to

Michael. 'Don't go to Mr. McKiley yet. We may need you. Wait with the car.' Then she took Shuan firmly by the arm in a grasp beneath which the girl flinched.

In the hall Joanna said with the sternness for which hysteria must call: 'Now tell me—what's happened? *And be quick!*'

'He—he was quiet until after I gave him his supper and sat with him. Then suddenly he shouted with pain. He sort of grimaced at me, and after that he couldn't talk for it. I tried to get Beltie and I couldn't. I tried to get Mums, but at the hotel in Belfast they didn't know where she was likely to be. I sent Cook down to the Dower House, and René has gone to Tulleen to get Beltie—his phone was out of order or something. But nothing I've been able to do for Roger has helped him—'

'Where is the pain?' Joanna was taking off her hat, her gloves.

'I don't know. Yes, I do—it's in his back—where he's never had it before—'

And Shuan, staring, did not understand the quiet, almost triumphant confidence with which Joanna turned towards the door of Roger's room. She had not Joanna's knowledge that she was going to help Roger, racked with present pain, but already freed from the death, the nothingness of the paralysis he had known.

★   ★   ★

For the rest of that night, when Dr. Beltane arrived at last to administer sedatives and to share her confident hopes, and throughout the next day Joanna had no thought nor time for anything other than her work with her patient.

It was not until the late evening that she realized with a shock that Dale was expecting her to go again to Dublin on the following day. Before they had parted at the Greville they had arranged that she should telephone him to tell him when to expect her. Now, of course, she could not go. That was quite definite. As she went to the telephone she wondered how Dale would take the news.

When she contacted him she said quickly: 'Dale, I'm dreadfully sorry, but I can't see you tomorrow. When I got back late last night—'

'Late?' queried Dale's voice. 'You weren't particularly late in leaving here.'

'No, but we ran out of petrol on the way—'

'Oh, come, Joanna, isn't that rather thin?' He sounded cold, suspicious.

Joanna was stung to indignation. 'It happens to be the truth,' she said shortly. 'Anyway, when I did get here I found that Mr. Carnehill's paralysis had begun to give way to pain—we hope it means that the feeling in his back is beginning to return. It's a sort of crisis and, of course, I can't leave him now.'

There was a pause. Then Dale asked: 'Are those his doctor's orders?'

'That I'm not to leave him? No. But obviously it's my duty not to.'

'Obviously—so far as it goes. But you don't particularly want to come to Dublin, do you?'

'Dale, what do you mean? Are you suggesting that I'm using Mr. Carnehill's illness as an excuse, or even that I'm lying about it?'

'No. I believe in it all right, just as I believe you are justified in deciding that you oughtn't to leave him. But I also believe you're glad not to have to come. *Aren't you?*'

Joanna rubbed a finger wearily above her brows. In an effort at jocularity she said: 'You're being awfully difficult, aren't you? You've never been like this before!'

'Neither have you!' came his swift retort. 'Joanna, do realize that I've known you for long enough to know that a strangeness has come over you—that for some reason, though I can only guess at it—you've grown away from me, even in this short time.'

Joanna caught her breath. She had not credited Dale with the perception that would tell him what she herself had realized—that they had indeed grown apart. Suddenly she wanted to deny it—to cling to that pleasant, undemanding relationship with him, which, before she came to Eire, had been an inseparable part of her life.

'That is absurd,' she said, not knowing that it was beyond the power of her sincerity to put real conviction into her voice. 'Do we have to argue about it? I'm very tired, and I think you're more than inclined to magnify something you've imagined—'

'I haven't imagined it. I've told you—I don't know what it is that I'm having to compete against, but there *is* something, that I'm convinced. Joanna will you do your best to get to Dublin tomorrow?'

'I can't, Dale! That's final. You know how I'm placed. Don't—don't make an issue of this!'

'I *am* making an issue of it. I must. If you won't come, then I shall come out to you, either tomorrow or the next day. I'd stay over in Eire on purpose, though I'm due back the day after tomorrow. If I come, you will see me, Joanna?'

'Yes. Yes—come if you must.' Joanna felt tired, dispirited and almost frightened as she replaced the receiver.

Mrs. Carnehill, back prematurely from Belfast, smiled kindly, if a trifle tiredly, when Joanna asked if it would be convenient for Dale to come out to Carrieghmere on the following day and for her to have an hour or two in which to be with him.

'Of course. Why not?' she said. 'He's your sweetheart in England, maybe? Ask him to stay for a meal, won't you?'

'Thank you. I will,' said Joanna, though she felt instinctively that Dale would refuse.

When she rang him up to come over he said quietly: 'Thank you. I'm glad you've been able to arrange it because I think it's time we said certain things to each other. And face to face is the only way in which they should be said.'

When Dale came, after one glance around the big drawing-room where she was waiting for him, he exclaimed: 'Heavens! Do we have to talk here?'

She said quickly: 'No, we go out into the park. I'll get my coat.'

In an awkward silence they went side by side across the deserted parkland, stooping beneath the deep boughs of the trees, now breaking reluctantly into bud. When they were at last out of sight of the house Dale stopped abruptly and said:

'Joanna, walking together or even being together at all today is only incidental to more important things—the things we have to say to each other. Perhaps we'd better get them said—'

She turned to face him, thrusting her hands deeply into the pockets of her travelling coat and being glad of the support of a gnarled bole as she looked frankly at him for almost the first time that day.

'Perhaps we had,' she agreed quietly.

Dale took a deep breath. 'Well, since it's you who've changed, perhaps you'd better begin. You've been different since you came over here. It—it fairly breathed through your letters. And even the day before yesterday you didn't want to come to Dublin to see me.'

'Yes, I did—'

'Only, I think, because you hoped that seeing me might help you to recapture something which you knew you'd lost. What was it, Joanna? Haven't I the right to know?'

She said nothing, feeling surprised for the second time at his insight into what had been happening to her. She felt that he was the good friend he had always been. If only, if only that could be enough!

He repeated: '*Haven't* I?'

'Yes, Dale. If there is anything ... I don't know—'

'There *is* something. Go on.'

'Well—I think that being apart from you this time *has* taught me something about—about us. We're very good friends, we've always enjoyed doing things together, but there isn't enough between us on which to—to store our hopes, our futures. We are still—strangers.'

Dale said slowly: 'This hasn't come about just through your coming over here. You believe you've fallen in love with another man. You think he has more to give you than I have—'

130

'*No!*' she denied sharply. 'No—not that!'

'What else am I to believe? Do you think that, since meeting him, I can't realize just why your letters, full of everything else about this benighted place made practically no reference to that man McKiley—?'

'It has nothing to do with McKiley. You must believe that!'

'How can I? You were happy enough when you left England, happy enough to take me as you found me. And I haven't been a mere cad, monopolizing your time for nothing. You've known all along what I've hoped for us—for our future!'

'Perhaps I've guessed. But you've never told me, Dale,' she reminded him gently.

He stared. 'Why should I have had to? You *must* have known!'

'I think—a woman needs telling.'

Dale said nothing. If he had held out his arms to her then, drawn her into them, she would have known that to the question in her heart there might be an answer in his. But he made no movement towards her as he muttered:

'All that romantic stuff! I never dreamt you had any time for it. Why must I make love to you, ask you in so many words—*as I'm doing now?*'

'You're asking me to marry you?'

'If that's what you want, yes. It's what I came today to do, anyway.'

131

'Did you?' Joanna caught at an ill-defined hope.

'Yes. I'd realized from your manner in Dublin and on the phone that you believed I'd failed you somewhere. So I said to myself, "All right. If it's marriage she wants, she shall have it—"

His voice held an ugly note, but he broke off at her protesting cry: 'Don't, Dale! You know it wasn't that—!'

'Then what was it? Why else did you see fit to use against me that man McKiley's attentions to you?'

'I'm not responsible for Justin McKiley's ideas on gallantry!' she rejected scornfully. 'And the very last thing I want is a proposal of marriage dragged from you at—at the pistol-point of something you think I'm demanding. I want to know that without the man I say I "love", *I* am nothing. And I want to know that I'm needed—as every woman must. Before I marry I've *got* to know all this. And between us, Dale—I'm sure of none of it!'

He said suddenly: 'Is that my fault?'

'It isn't a question of "fault", Dale! We're good friends. I hope we always may be—'

'And "Thank God we found out before it was too late", I suppose?' His tone held bitterness, and he paused before he said: 'Well, will you marry me, Joanna, or won't you?'

132

'The answer is "No", Dale. It must be. One day you'll be grateful to me—when you've found the "real thing" yourself.'

'So this, Joanna, is goodbye?' He held out his hand.

She took it, and through stiff lips said: 'Yes. It's better so.' Even then Dale might have appealed to some hunger in her—some desire to serve, to be needed, to be *loved*. But he only dropped her hand and turned away.

CHAPTER NINE

Gradually as the reluctant Irish spring advanced, Roger Carnehill began to find strength where there had been complete atrophy and peace where he had known pain. But neither Dr. Beltane nor his Dublin surgeon would allow him to rest on the laurels, so to speak, of this partial recovery.

'You've got to work for it, young man!' Dr. Beltane adjured him. 'Exercises—and more exercises—and no shirking possible, because Nurse Merivale'll be superintending every minute of 'em!'

So every morning Roger, bored but reasonably submissive, stretched and flexed his stiffened legs and made archways of the spine that was beginning to respond again to his will.

'Kindergarten stuff!' he would grumble to the quiet tone of Joanna's: 'One—two—relax!' And she would smile at him, but would insist upon the steady rhythm being kept up.

At last he said: 'Look here, can't you abandon this metronome business? I've got the idea now—in fact I dream "One—two—relax" o' nights. Why shouldn't we talk instead, and you can pull me up if I start slacking?'

Joanna agreed, knowing that if he became too bored he would not try. But after a little desultory conversation as he worked he said suddenly: 'This is too silly too. How can I talk while I'm going up and down like the coils of a sea-serpent? *You* talk to me. Tell me things—'

'What sort of things?' smiled Joanna.

'Oh—things. Anything, so long as I don't have to say "Really?" at the top of an arch or "Is that so?" at the bottom! Tell me—tell me about when you were a little girl!'

The *naïveté* of this request took Joanna by complete surprise. Of what possible interest could her childhood be to him? But the memory of it, happy though money-restricted, was vividly with her, and she found it easy to talk about it to him. It became a kind of saga which ran on from day to day, to which Roger listened intently, even correcting details of it here and there.

And when he reached the stage of being able to sit in a wheel-chair by the window before being settled down for the night, he began to tell her about his own boyhood, of his hated schooldays in the North—'among the Orangemen'—as he called them; of his passionate homesickness for Carrieghmere through eight months of the year, and the wild delight of possessing and being possessed by it during the other four.

'When my father died,' he said one night, 'I vowed I'd give the rest of my life to Carrieghmere and all it stood for. But since all this happened I've had to let go—or rather, have it wrested from me. The running of it has virtually gone to McKiley, and now Mother has fogged the issue with this fool idea of journalism. A *Carnehill*—a journalist!'

Joanna thought it best to change the subject. 'You'll take the reins again soon. The estate will be yours once more.'

'Yes.' He added thoughtfully: 'It'll have been more than two years. I wonder whether the reins one goes to take up are at all the same as one believed one laid down? Whether I shall find that Carrieghmere has marched ahead without me? You know, I'm going to be half afraid of that—?'

'Nothing can have changed much in two years,' Joanna assured him. 'And nearly all invalids have that fear at some time or another that they're not going to like taking

135

up their responsibilities again.'

He glanced at her obliquely. 'Of course. I forgot. Even my personal reactions aren't my own. They simply occupy a line or two in that "official" case-book which you claim you don't keep!'

*   *   *

The kitchen of Carrieghmere was a pleasant place. It was frequently warmer than the rest of the house, for one thing. Mrs. Carnehill would often be there, experimenting with recipes, and the more recherché scents of her cookery would mingle with the homely smell of cabbage and boiling bacon from which the kitchen places of Irish houses never quite escape.

This evening Mrs. Carnehill was not there. But Shuan was, and so were Michael and René Menden.

Shuan was moodily digging grease from a crack in the table with the point of a knife. Michael sat saddle-wise across a chair, his arms folded upon the back of it. René stood, very upright, at Shuan's side, looking down at her bent head.

Michael was saying: 'Sure, an' he can't be doin' it to ye, Miss Shuan. Wasn't I tellin' himself so, this very day?'

Shuan flung down the knife and looked up, pushing her fingers into the hair at each side of her face in a way that was very much her own.

'That's what I don't know,' she said. 'He didn't consult me—he *told* me!'

René said: 'I think he cannot have the power—'

And Joanna put in gently: 'What's the matter? May I know?'

They reacted characteristically. René bowed in her direction, Shuan took up the knife and went on with her excavations and Michael touched a cap which wasn't there.

''Tis the terrible trouble Miss Shuan is in—' he began. But Shuan put in:

'It's not terrible trouble. It's just—awkward.' And Joanna thought, 'It's always the same with her. Except for that night of Roger's crisis when she couldn't do anything but turn to me for help, it's as if she's impelled to tone down everything she feels because she can't bear to accept sympathy from me.'

Michael accepted the check in good part. ''Tis Mr. McKiley. He has told Miss Shuan that he has had a good offer for the mare she had set her heart on training for the Horse Show.'

For the moment, thinking absently in terms of a local fête, Joanna asked innocently: 'Which Horse Show?'

She might have committed high treason. Even René looked pityingly at her and Shuan

137

replied scornfully:

'The *Dublin* Horse Show, of course. In August.'

'But whose mare is it?' asked Joanna bewilderedly.

'She's ours. We bred her here. And she's got a first-rate chance, no matter whether Michael or I rode her.'

'Then surely Mr. McKiley—?'

'He says he's got a duty to the place. That an excellent offer isn't to be turned down for the sake of what he calls the "off-chance" of her taking a prize at the Show. I can't make him see that the *honour* alone—'

'But it can't be a question for Mr. McKiley to decide,' protested Joanna. 'If the mare is Carrieghmere property a decision like that must rest with Mr. Carnehill.' She turned to René. 'Oughtn't you or Mrs. Carnehill to speak to him about it? Or—or would you like me to?'

She had been looking at René, and nothing had prepared her for Shuan's passionate denial. The girl's face flamed as she exclaimed: 'You'll do nothing of the kind! I'll not have Roger's help asked for the sake of any horse, mare or foal on the place! *Nor* for my sake! I'll fight this out with Justin myself. If he insists on selling Deirdre I'll have to make-do with one of the second-raters. But I'll not have *anyone* whining to Roger for me on account of any horseflesh in Ireland!'

Joanna was so taken aback that her tone was rather cold as she replied: 'You seem to forget that Mr. McKiley appears to be proposing to sell Mr. Carnehill's property without his consent, and that your feelings don't matter, except to you, one way or the other.'

'But he couldn't do it if he hadn't Roger's consent. If not about Deirdre in particular, obviously he knows he has the right to judge for himself about buying or selling for the estate. Otherwise he wouldn't *dare* to do it. But I'll *not* have Roger appealed to!'

Joanna said nothing, feeling that about Justin's authority to act upon his own judgment she was probably right.

René said gently: 'I myself will speak to Mr. McKiley—' And though Shuan replied moodily: 'There's nothing *you* can do, René,' the glance she gave him was newly kind and friendly, and Joanna saw the young man flush with pleasure.

'And which of the others would ye put into training if Deirdre goes, Miss Shuan?' Michael was asking.

'I don't know. Tansie or Lady of Belmont, I suppose. What do you think?'

Michael levered himself from the chair. 'Could ye spare a scattered minute now, the way we'd be lookin' at the both of them in their boxes?'

Shuan rose. But before she left the kitchen

with the stable-lad she said to René: 'Are you coming too?'

He nodded eagerly. But when the other two had gone he lingered a moment with Joanna. He said: 'She is—brusque, little Shuan. But by it she means nothing. In reality she has—has got?—no, I do not understand the English "got"—she has the heart of gold!'

Joanna nodded and smiled. With a sort of warm glow at her own heart she was thinking: 'I'm glad René *can* love Shuan like that—seeing her faults, accepting them and yet loving her all the same. Because, even if she gives him nothing in return he'll suffer, but ultimately he'll not lose anything.'

When she went back to Roger's room she was sorely tempted to break Shuan's confidence and tell him about the proposed sale of the mare, Deirdre. But she found it difficult not to believe that at least in a general way the whole thing had his consent. And the girl had been so passionate in her determination not to appeal to him that Joanna said nothing. If he did not know of it already, sooner or later he would hear of it from Mrs. Carnehill or McKiley. And it was really no business of hers.

A few days later she heard from René that the sale had gone through.

'Shuan hasn't said anything about it,' she told him, making a mental reservation of:

'She wouldn't—to me!' 'What does she feel about it, do you think?'

He hesitated. 'She is brave. She says little. But I think she has begun to—hate Justin McKiley.'

Joanna thought it best not to discuss this side of the matter with René. Perhaps, as Dale had suggested, she had already become too deeply involved in the 'personalities' of Carrieghmere. One day she must leave it all behind her. When Roger really began to move about and to take up the threads again, that day would not be far off. And for her own sake she could not allow Carrieghmere and the people in it to lay too great a hold upon her life.

So she said only: 'I dare say she has begun to train one of the other mares she mentioned?'

'Yes. The Lady of Belmont. She has asked me to help with the training.' He sighed. 'She would not allow it, but I cannot believe that Mr. Carnehill would have permitted the mare Deirdre to be sold if he had known—'

Joanna sighed too. 'Well, there it is, René. Shuan had evidently made up her mind about it and it's too late now. You can help her best now by encouraging her with Lady of Belmont—making her accept Mr. McKiley's challenge by *determining* to win!'

René smiling faintly. 'Shuan knows more about horses than I shall ever know. I cannot hope to make her believe anything if she does not know it for herself. But I will help her—*mais sans doute!*'

★   ★   ★

Every morning very early Shuan, accompanied faithfully by René, had Lady of Belmont out for exercise upon the springy turf of the bog land. Shuan declared she was pleased with the way the mare was shaping, and one day, shyly and diffidently, she came to Joanna to ask if she would temporarily take back the coveted duty of taking Roger's morning tea to him.

'I can get out with René earlier, so,' she explained.

Joanna, smiling agreement, said: 'With René?'

Shuan flushed. 'Well, with Lady of Belmont of course! But René always comes, and he has to be back at work at half-eight. It isn't that I don't want to take Roger's tea. Or that I want longer in bed, if that's what you're thinking!'

'It isn't,' replied Joanna quietly. 'Besides, you're not as worried about Mr. Carnehill as you were, are you? You *are* quite happy about him now?'

A look of alarm flashed into the girl's eyes. She gulped as she said quickly: 'Yes. Yes, of course. Why, aren't you? He is getting better,

142

isn't he? There's nothing going wrong *now*?'

'Nothing at all, I hope,' Joanna assured her. But the memory of that look of fear in Shuan's eyes remained with her for a long time.

Meanwhile she was surprised and rather ashamed of the ease with which the memory of Dale Woodward had slipped from her consciousness. True, since that last meeting with him she had been almost too busy to think of personal things. And he had not attempted to write to her again, nor she to him.

All memory of him was fading. Not only the memory of the ugly things about him—his jealousy, his unreasonable possessiveness over something—herself—which he had never found it necessary to claim as his own, but all the other, pleasanter things about their friendship, their easy acceptance of each other and the casual, desultory conversation which had been frequently all they had found necessary.

That Dale must feel the same was proved by a letter she received, a couple of months after his visit to Eire, from a friend of hers at the Marrone Nursing Home.

After a page or two of satisfying gossip and shop, Sister Allitsen wrote:

'By the way, what did you do to Dale Woodward on his visit to Eire? Before that, he would sometimes waylay one or other of us to ask what news we had of you. But since then—silence of the most profound!

'And now Carrick—her brother works in the same laboratory as Dale, you know—says he's engaged to a new girl assistant they have in the lab. Did you know about this? Even if you didn't I don't feel terribly "puss puss" about telling you, because you know, Joanna dear, that I always doubted that you and Dale were suited to each other. Actually, I can't help but be a little glad ... Don't be angry with me. I only know that I felt in my bones that there wasn't the "real" thing between you. And I knew—for you'd told me—that he had never given you the chance to *be* real. He had never asked you to be his wife.

'Now, it seems, he has asked this other girl. Don't be too hurt about it, Joanna. And one day, tell me as much about it as you feel you'd like me to know.'

Joanna folded the letter, feeling grateful for Joan Allitsen's disinterested friendship. She remembered Dale's own reference to his new assistant—'easy on the eyes but dumb'—that was how he had described her to Joanna. Perhaps, even then, he had been guilty of the thing of which he had accused *her*—of being over-casual on purpose in her references to Justin McKiley. But she dismissed the thought as unworthy. Dale, in his fashion, had at least been sincere. Now, in this other girl, he had found consolation and his own 'reality'. *His* answer to the eternal question between men and women was not, and now would never be—'Joanna'.

★   ★   ★

And so the day came when Roger was to leave his room for the first time.

Everyone was there. Dr. Beltane, beaming and rubbing his hands, Mrs. Carnehill, her blue eyes unnaturally bright and her high colour paler than usual, Shuan, hovering nervously, and in the background Roseen and Cook, clutching each other by the arms and spasmodically giggling.

Joanna bent to tuck a corner of the rug about Roger's legs as he sat in the wheel-chair which she was about to push out on to the terrace.

'You know, I've got the most depressing sense of anti-climax!' he said in a low voice.

'You mean you've waited so long for this, now it doesn't seem to mean very much after all?' she smiled up at him.

'Yes, that, perhaps. And perhaps'—he glanced about the room which had been his prison for more than two years—'I realize that I'm leaving a kingdom where I've ruled, for a strange country where maybe I no longer signify!'

Joanna shook her head. 'I think,' she said quietly, 'that you'll find you signify again very soon!' Then she wheeled the chair out on to the terrace where the others were waiting.

Beyond the corner of the house lay a view of the surrounding park which Roger had not been able to command from his bed. He heaved himself up in the chair in order to see it better. And with his eyes fixed upon the sharply outlined shadows of the grass he breathed quietly: 'Bless it. It goes on—and on.'

No one spoke, respecting the moment in which he and his heritage were alone together. Then suddenly, as if she could control herself no longer, Shuan stumbled forward to fall upon her knees at the side of his chair and to burst into a storm of sobs.

Startled, he looked down at her bent head. Mrs. Carnehill cried: 'Shuan, don't distress Roger!' But it was Joanna who stooped to put an arm about the sobbing girl in order to draw her to her feet.

Evidently Shuan did not know what she was doing, for she turned her bent head to hide it upon Joanna's shoulder and went on crying softly.

Joanna kept her arm about her while she urged softly: 'Shuan, we know how much it has mattered to you. But it's all right now. You simply can't give way like this when all

146

along you've been so brave!'

Shuan did not answer, being occupied, like a child, in controlling her tears. When she lifted her head at last she stood irresolutely by Joanna's side, smiling tremulously down at Roger, who summoned an enormous wink and a grimace.

Then Dr. Beltane strode firmly across to her, took her round the waist.

'Now you, my gossoon,' he ordered, 'are going to take me round to the stables to find Michael. There's a small matter of a gasket in my car—'

She turned obediently. When they had gone Mrs. Carnehill said: 'She is overwrought, poor child. She has minded so much—too much.'

And Roger, who had sometimes appeared impatient of or embarrassed by Shuan's extravagances of expression, said with unexpected gentleness: 'Bless her. She'd have stood it all for me if she'd been able—and more besides.'

During the brief hour or two of his permitted outing there was only one other discordant note. And that was when Justin McKiley came striding up from the Dower House.

The two men looked at each other. Then upon a light note Justin said:

'Congratulations, old man. "Monarch of all you survey" again at last?'

'Thanks,' said Roger coldly. 'I hope so!'

And the hostility between them was something which could almost be felt.

★   ★   ★

That night Shuan went to bed early, leaving Mrs. Carnehill and Joanna alone together after dinner. Presently Mrs. Carnehill went on her nightly visit to Roger, and when she returned Joanna thought she looked oddly tired and distressed.

'Mrs. Carnehill, you've taken a lot of strain,' said Joanna gently. 'May I pour you some more coffee?—it's still hot. Or would you rather go to bed with a sedative which I could mix for you?'

Roger's mother turned strangely haunted eyes upon her. 'No,' she said. 'I'm all right.' But the emptily twisting hands in her lap belied her words.

'You're worried about Mr. Carnehill?' Joanna sat down beside her. 'There's no need—'

'Not about his condition. Not any more. But oh, Joanna, you've not an idea at all of the way I've hoped for and prayed for and—dreaded this day—!'

'*Dreaded*?' The word had a secret echo in Joanna's own heart. But she must not think of that now...

'Yes. I've known it had to come. Already

he's asking questions—and I can't put off the answering of them any longer. He insists now on having an account of our stewardship— mine and Justin's. And—and that's something that I can scarcely bear to tell him!'

CHAPTER TEN

There was silence in the room, broken only by the ticking of the grandfather clock and the intermittent creak of an old tree beyond the window.

Joanna said gently, laying her hand upon the older woman's: 'I think I've known for a long time that there was something you were unhappy about. Would it help to tell me more?'

Mrs. Carnehill withdrew one of her hands in order to twist restlessly at the string of pearls round her throat. 'Yes—yes. I suppose it would. I've been so worried. Though it isn't as if—as if anyone had done anything *wrong*, do you understand—?' she said rather pitifully.

'You mean you've been worried about the way the estate's affairs have gone since your son's accident? Is that it?'

'Yes. It has been going downhill ever since then. There's never enough money now for anything—look at the state of the park wall, and the stables are just as bad—And yet market prices haven't altered much, so I just don't know why! And all Justin says is that it's "inevitable" or that it's "just a passing fluctuation". He doesn't try to make it very clear, and I'm afraid I'm rather stupid.'

'Well, perhaps it is inevitable,' suggested Joanna thoughtfully. 'The place had a complete change of management when Mr. McKiley took over.'

Mrs. Carnehill clutched at the idea as at a straw. 'Yes that's what I hoped it might be. But'—doubtfully—'that ought to have righted itself by now, wouldn't you think? Justin has been in charge for two years. Even with his different methods—'

'Yes, you'd think so,' agreed Joanna. 'Besides, I suppose you have auditors? You—you don't suspect anything wrong— really wrong, I mean?'

'No. What would there be? Justin's accounts are all right. It's simply that Carrieghmere doesn't seem to pay its way any more.'

'But if this is so,' urged Joanna, 'oughtn't you to have let Mr. Carnehill know? The place is his, and I believe that for a long time he has been anxious to take back at least some of his responsibilities towards it. You've known it too, haven't you?'

'Yes—only too well. But, you see, in the

beginning Justin had to take over completely—they wouldn't let me bring to Roger anything which might have worried him. Then, later, I didn't want to consult him lest it should bring on a relapse. Later still, I haven't wanted him to guess at all what has been happening. I've known how antagonistic he and Justin are to each other and I haven't dared to let things come to a real clash between them, for we couldn't afford to lose Justin while Roger was so ill. So I've encouraged Justin to give him only general reports, hoping from month to month that things would right themselves. But they didn't. And because I couldn't sell anything—pictures or furniture or silver—without Roger's consent, I had to try to make money in the only way open to me—'

'By your journalism?' asked Joanna.

'Yes. And Roger has made no secret of how he has hated *that*. But I was lucky. I had been dabbling in it for a long time as a hobby, and when the need arose I was fortunate enough to get several regular commissions. The money has helped a lot, but you do see why I've never been able to meet Roger's arguments against it? The alternative would have been to sell things which ultimately he would have missed. These, for instance'—again her fingers strayed to her pearls—'which are Carnehill heirlooms and which I couldn't part with.'

'You could have told him the truth,' said Joanna slowly. 'He wouldn't have blamed you.'

Mrs. Carnehill said: 'Blame, is it? Would I have cared about his blame if I had thought that to tell him would not set him back hopelessly from recovery—?'

'That was earlier,' Joanna reminded her gently. 'Now it can't hurt him physically to learn that he will be returning to something different from that which he left. In fact, now he must be told. For very soon he will be able to get about and see for himself.'

'Yes, I realize that,' said the older woman wretchedly. 'But it's the harder for having put it off for so long—'

'I think—I could tell him,' put in Joanna. 'In fact, he'll scarcely need telling. For I believe he knows.'

'He knows?'

'"Guesses" might have been a better word. For a long time he's worried more about what has been kept from him than he could have done over the truth, Mrs. Carnehill. Forgive my saying this now. Perhaps you feel I should have said it before, but until you spoke to me I couldn't very well interfere.'

Mrs. Carnehill looked at her gratefully. 'Bless you, Joanna,' she said. 'I wish I'd had a daughter like you! Do you mean you'd prepare him for the facts which Justin and I will have to put before him sooner or later?'

'Yes. If he needs preparation—which I doubt. Lately we've talked about a lot of things—among them, the picking up of threads, the re-shouldering of responsibility. In certain moods he dreads the thought; in others, increasingly as he gets stronger, he is ready to face anything that lies in front.'

A note of quiet, confident belief in Roger's character had crept into Joanna's voice as she spoke. She did not know that something else shone behind her eyes—something which Mrs. Carnehill, watching her, vaguely sensed, but as yet did not understand. She said again: 'Bless you!' And then added, half-enviously but without bitterness: 'Almost I could believe that you know my own son better than I do myself!'

Joanna did not answer. She did not know herself how it was that she could speak so confidently of Roger's reactions to a future she would not be there to see. She knew now that, for a different reason from his mother's, she too had dreaded this day—the day that marked the first step towards his needing her no more. In the re-blossoming of Carrieghmere under his guidance there would be no room for Nurse Joanna Merivale of London. As a 'case' she would have done with Roger Carnehill; she would have had to learn to forget him—*as a man*.

For a moment the thought meant nothing to her reason. It was her heart which took the significance of it in a cold spear-thrust of pain.

As in a dream she heard Mrs. Carnehill saying anxiously: 'Joanna, you've gone suddenly white! We work you too hard, to be sure! But we've come to lean upon you so much—all of us! But you must take things more easily now. Presently, as Roger gets stronger, you'll be able to begin to enjoy Carrieghmere—'

The bland assumption that for a long time to come she would be there to 'enjoy' the place was something with which Joanna longed with every fibre to agree. But through dry lips she said:

'Soon there'll be no need for my staying on any longer. Time, then, will be all the nursing Mr. Carnehill will need. Dr. Beltane will judge, of course. But—a week or two, perhaps—' (That was the brief measure of bitter-sweetness left to her still. A week or two more. And then—nothing.)

*   *   *

Though there was now a magic in simply being with him, in the days which followed Joanna often found it difficult to meet Roger's eyes and to keep her hitherto disciplined hands from trembling as they went about their prosaic tasks. But in the end it was the very discipline of her profession which told

154

her that for as long as Roger Carnehill had need of her skill she must give it as freely and as impersonally as ever.

Even so, discipline found it difficult to control every movement of her hands, her eyes, every inflection of her voice during those awkward days. And though she told herself it might be her imagination, Roger himself seemed to have changed. As he grew stronger and able to do more things for himself he took on a new dignity which seemed no longer to need to armour itself against the world by an indulgence in caprice and self-pity. Roger Carnehill, returning slowly to man's estate, was above all things a man...

Once, when they sat together on the terrace and she had supposed him to be reading, she looked up quickly to find his eyes deeply concentrated upon her face. Momentarily there seemed to be in them a question...

As she had expected, he took the tale of Carrieghmere's difficulties without surprise, almost without dismay.

He said only: 'I've known for a long time, of course, that Mother has been hiding something—for my sake, as she thought, poor dear. Though why she couldn't have given me a hint before the thing became a landslide—'

'At first they wouldn't let her,' Joanna pointed out. 'Then I suppose it began to look like gross mismanagement, and inasmuch as it was that, she felt she had let you down.'

'If it's mismanagement, that's McKiley's pigeon,' argued Roger with a new grim set to his lips. 'If Mother had only let me at him—!'

'But that, for good or ill is something which, all along, she has tried to avoid—a clash between the two of you, which would have meant that Justin McKiley would have to go. She believed it best to let matters go on, hoping they would right themselves as he assured her they would, and trying to close the gap in her own way.'

'M'm.' It was typical of the new Roger that, even to Joanna, he would no longer indulge in irritable criticism of Mrs. Carnehill's work. For a moment there was silence. Then he snapped: 'How well have *you* come to know McKiley since you've been here?'

The abruptness of the question so took Joanna aback that she flushed and stammered almost guiltily: 'N-not very well. Why?'

'But you've come to know something of him?' he persisted. 'Joanna'—there was almost a note of pleading in his voice where earlier there would have been truculence—'there's no need to continue indefinitely the Tell Roger Nothing theory, you know!'

Because she dared not defend herself as she would have wished, Joanna could only say evenly: 'I'm not keeping anything from you. I *don't* know Mr. McKiley very well. He's been to dinner with Mrs. Carnehill and the rest of us several times. He drove me back from Dublin on the day I went with you to the nursing home. And on—another occasion he took me in and brought me out from Dublin. Once I went to a party of his at the Dower House—'

'You did? I didn't know that?'

'You weren't here. It was on the first day I mentioned. He gave me lunch at the Sheldon, drove me home and asked me on the way to go to the party in the evening.'

'And you went?'

'Yes. It was just an ordinary cocktail affair—'

'I see.' There was a world of withheld comment in his tone, but just what such comment referred to Joanna could not guess.

There was a pause. When Roger spoke again it was with a studied lightness that he said:

'Well, it took Justin to introduce us to the cocktail party here at Carrieghmere! In my day we went in for something more robust in the way of entertainment. We shall again—' Then he went on more seriously: 'Joanna, don't you see that I've got to try to be just to the fellow, if only for Mother's sake, because she believes that he is doing his best? But also, very soon, I've got to try to find what he's been doing with my affairs. For more

157

than two years he has been free to fell my timber, sell my stock, rule my tenants and conduct a private life about which I know very little. I realize that the last is my concern only so far as it may affect the rest. But if I find it does affect the rest—'

'You mean,' said Joanna slowly, 'that you think he may have been using his position at Carrieghmere in some way?'

'I don't know. How could I?' retorted Roger with something of his old irritability. 'I only know that he drives the sort of car we've never been able to afford, throws expensive parties and keeps rather—exotic company. In particular, there's a woman—Magda Somebody. René has mentioned her.'

'Yes, I've met her,' Joanna told him. 'At the party and later in Dublin.'

'And she is his sort?'

'Essentially so, I should say.' For a moment Joanna was deeply tempted to try to express what she thought and instinctively felt about Justin McKiley.

But she realized that in seeking to deal with Justin with scrupulous fairness, Roger needed facts about the man—facts uncluttered by the feminine prejudice which was all she could bring to her judgment of him.

She did not know, of course, what passed between Roger and his mother in their first long talk after that, nor the details of the even longer interview between Roger and his

158

agent. But after the latter Roger commented: 'I suppose, as I begin to take over, only time is going to tell whether the fellow has been twisting us or not. I thought perhaps he wouldn't be able to produce figures. But he can, and except that everything he buys costs more and everything he sells brings in less, there doesn't seem much wrong with them. What am I to do?'

'Wait,' counselled Joanna. 'If he's really loyal and honest you might serve Carrieghmere badly by doing anything hastily. If he isn't, you must still give yourself time to prove a case against him. Does that sound good sense to you?' she added with a smile.

Roger made a wry grimace. 'Uncommonly so, though it's advice I'm reluctant to take. Because I don't like the man you don't know how I long to make a clean sweep of him and all his works! But until I can take over completely myself or, as you say, prove a case against him, I realize that would be an insane thing entirely. Joanna—!' Suddenly, surprisingly, he reached for her hand, gripped it within his own as he repeated: 'Joanna, when shall I be free—*really* free?'

Her hand was locked in his and for a moment she let it lie there, making-believe ... Then she turned it gently and he released it. And all the infinite tenderness she felt for him was masked by a nurse's solicitude as she said quietly: 'A few weeks now—no more.'

*　　*　　*

It had been as difficult to meet Shuan's eyes as to meet Roger's, in those first days of her knowledge of her love for him. For where, before, it had been merely her skill which had usurped the girl's place with him, now every moment spent with him appeared to Joanna's conscience as a cruel cheating of Shuan's rights.

But Shuan was changing too ... She appeared increasingly to have her own secrets.

She spent a great deal more time out of doors with her dogs and the horses and upon other activities about the estate, sometimes in René's company, but, as he himself admitted, not always. Once when he had mentioned to Mrs. Carnehill that Justin McKiley would be away for the day and that he would be solely at the mercy of Mrs. Hagerty's cooking, he had been invited to take his meals at Carrieghmere, where he duly and punctually appeared for luncheon.

Roger, Mrs. Carnehill, and Joanna were there too. But Shuan was not.

'Where can the child be?' queried Mrs. Carnehill. 'Have you seen anything of her this morning, René?'

René looked surprised. 'We rode before

breakfast, yes. I left her at half-past eight. But did she not tell you? She has gone to Dublin with Mr. McKiley—'

'To Dublin?' exclaimed Mrs. Carnehill, 'and—'

'With McKiley?' echoed Roger.

'I am sorry. I thought you would know,' said René uncomfortably.

Mrs. Carnehill quickly recovered her poise, and Joanna was forced to admire the effort she made to protect the girl's dignity before René. She glanced at Roger and said quietly: 'Now I remember—she did say something about being out. I must have misunderstood her. You know how I get things muddled—'

Roger, however, seemed constrained to make no such effort. He turned to René to ask coldly: 'I don't understand about this. Do you mean you thought we should know about her having gone to Dublin because she does go about with McKiley normally? That it's a usual thing for her to do? That she does it often?'

Mrs. Carnehill interposed: 'Roger! René couldn't possibly know!'

'I dare say he does,' was the dry reply. 'After all, I thought Shuan was usually out with him—when she wasn't alone. I, at least, didn't know she was making a companion of McKiley!'

Hesitantly René said: 'Lately it has been so, I think. He has seemed to seek her out.

161

She has come to the Dower House—'

'I see,' Roger said quietly. And a brooding, charged silence fell upon them all.

Later René sought out Joanna when she was alone.

'Mr. Carnehill is angry about Shuan,' he said unnecessarily. 'But indeed it is nothing! Will you assure him of that? *Bien compris*—it is understandable—yes?—that Shuan, a lovely girl, should be a little flattered for a time by the attentions of a man like Mr. McKiley. He is—skilful with women, *n'est-ce pas?*'

Joanna shivered involuntarily, remembering the man's attempted 'skill' with herself. She hoped not, but it was indeed possible that Shuan was intrigued by him, as she had been. And yet there was something she did not understand...

She said slowly: 'But René, do you remember, after Mr. McKiley had sold Deirdre the mare and Shuan was so upset about it, you told me that you thought she had come to hate him for it? If that were so—only a little while ago—how has *this* happened since?'

René scraped at the ground with the toe of his shoe. 'I thought so. Perhaps I was wrong. Perhaps—I flattered myself and I do not understand her as well as I believed—'

★　　★　　★

At dinner Shuan's name was not mentioned, and shortly after the meal René excused himself to return to the Dower House.

Mrs. Carnehill let him go without suggesting that he should wait to see Shuan. And it was not until an hour or two later that the girl herself appeared.

Her face was flushed and there was a new, artificial jauntiness in her manner. She put an arm lightly around Roger's shoulders, and her greetings of 'Hullo, darlings' seemed to include them all in it. But Joanna noticed that her eyes were watchful and her gaiety was on the defensive. She was hiding something...

Mrs. Carnehill said in a matter-of-fact tone: 'What about dinner, darling? Have you had any?'

'Heavens, yes. Ages ago. Justin took me to the Greville. It was marvellous. We had—' For a moment the natural Shuan seemed about to break through with an artless catalogue of the meal's highlights. But the new, wary Shuan substituted instead: 'We had quite a party. Justin's friend Magda was there, and some men Justin knows—'

'In fact, a party that you might have mentioned here you meant to attend!' It was Roger's first contribution to the conversation and his voice was cold.

Shuan swung round upon him. 'I don't see why!' she retorted defensively. 'Mums

163

doesn't usually question where I'm going. After all, I'm not a child any more, being expected to report every movement—And if it's a question of my not being here for two meals, well *they're* not usually so punctual that—'

'It's not a question of meals, punctual or otherwise. And you know it,' put in Roger icily. 'It's merely a question of common courtesy and—of the company you choose!'

'Oh, you mean *Justin?*' The pert affectation of surprise was offensive, and Joanna realized from a glance at his darkening face that Roger found it so.

'Yes, I do mean McKiley,' he said crisply. 'And I'd rather you didn't associate with him, that's all.'

Shuan began stormily: 'It's not for you to say—' at the same moment as Mrs. Carnehill murmured:

'Roger, aren't we getting things rather out of proportion? Justin is our agent and presumably has our confidence. Shuan and he have known each other for a long time. There's no reason at all why he shouldn't want to take her about—'

'Nor any reason at all why she should find it necessary to accept!' he snapped. Then with an air of considering the incident closed, he rose, picked up the stick which he must still use for walking, and moved towards the door.

Shuan's jaunty affectation dropped from her like a fallen cloak.

She said in a small, tight voice: 'Roger, wait!'

But he had already gone, and after staring for a moment at the closed door she turned back, her whole figure seeming to droop with frustration.

'There was no particular harm in your going to Dublin with Justin, darling,' said Mrs. Carnehill gently. 'But you know that Roger has never liked him, and he does tend to get things out of proportion because of it.'

Shuan shrugged her arms out of her coat and let it drop over the back of a chair. Then she sat down on a low stool, hugging her knees and not looking at anyone.

'It's not what you think!' she said. 'It's—well, Justin knows a lot of people, and he may be able to find me a job!'

Joanna looked at her sharply. Something—perhaps the momentary hesitation before the bald statement—gave her to believe that Shuan, realizing that some explanation of her association with Justin was called for, had offered this one on the spur of the moment.

But Mrs. Carnehill took it at its face value. 'A *job*, Shuan! What sort of a job? You hadn't said anything to me about wanting one!'

Shuan jerked an ungracious head towards Joanna.

'It was her suggestion in the first place. She

165

said she thought I had taste in interior decoration—antiques and things—and asked me if I'd ever thought about taking it up as a career. I said no, and that you and Roger would have a fit at the very idea. But afterwards I thought I'd like to, and I asked her how to go about getting one.'

Mrs. Carnehill looked bewilderedly at Joanna. 'Neither of you mentioned it to me!'

'I didn't realize,' Joanna told her quietly, 'that Shuan was going to take up seriously a suggestion I made quite casually. I didn't think it was ever mentioned to you, Mrs. Carnehill, because Shuan didn't seem anxious to go on with the idea when—when she realized the practical difficulties in the way—getting regularly to Dublin or even farther afield, for instance—'

'And now you are thinking of it again?' Mrs. Carnehill turned to Shuan. 'Darling, do you think you'd really *like* it? And what does Justin know about it, anyway?'

Shuan shrugged her shoulders, and Joanna was reminded painfully of Roger abandoning a subject in which he had lost interest. But she knew from observation of the girl while they had been talking, that Shuan was seeking to shrug off as of no consequence a topic which she had used only as a cloak for something else. She said vaguely: 'I don't know. But he has a lot of influence with people in Dublin. And he *says* he knows of just the thing for me, but it may take time.'

Mrs. Carnehill regarded her niece in a puzzled way. 'I can't think—' she was beginning, when at the door there was a sudden diversion. Roseen the housemaid appeared unceremoniously at it, her head completely wrapped about turban-wise with a printed cotton square and her eyes wide with horror.

'Could ye come now to the kitchen, Ma'am?' she begged Mrs. Carnehill. 'For will Cook not have the scalp off me when she comes back from spending the evening with her mother, the way she laid upon me the solemn promise to take a pair of ducks from the oven the minute they were done?'

Mrs. Carnehill rose. 'And you've burnt them, I dare say?' she said tolerantly.

'Black! Black as the craggy hearthstone!' declared Roseen with dramatic relish. 'Would ye come now and see could we maybe *scrape* the creatures, so that Cook might be thinking they had no more than the breath of an overheating in the oven?'

To this impassioned appeal Mrs. Carnehill could do no less than yield. She left the room with Roseen, and Joanna, wanting to laugh looked across at Shuan, hoping to share the joke.

But the girl's eyes were fixed upon hers without humour. Rather breathlessly she said: 'You knew I was making it up, didn't

167

you? That it wasn't the real reason for—for Justin?'

'Yes, I think I guessed.' Joanna's tone was quiet as she added: 'But does there have to be a reason "for Justin", as you put it? Forgive me, Shuan, but I think you're being terribly unwise!'

The girl's mouth set in a stubborn line. 'That's my affair. I know what I'm doing.'

'Do you? Well, my idea of Justin McKiley is that he is a very knowledgeable man of the world and that he could be—quite unscrupulous for his own ends, whatever they happened to be. And doesn't it weigh with you that Mr. Carnehill hates the idea of your associating with him? *Must* you go on—for any reason at all?'

For answer Shuan gave a short, rather mirthless laugh. Then she reached for her discarded coat and flung it over one shoulder with a flick of the wrist. Before she left the room she said over her shoulder: 'Yes, I'm afraid I must. Only I couldn't hope that anyone would understand!'

And Joanna, alone and infinitely puzzled, found only one rather incredible suspicion dawning upon her. Was it possible—was it *anyhow* possible that Shuan believed she could stimulate Roger's love by making him jealous of Justin McKiley?

Desperately, without thought for herself and her own love for Roger, Joanna longed to be able to make Shuan see, irrevocably, that she could gain nothing in that way—nothing! That jealousy, deliberately created, was a boomerang, inflicting most hurt where it originally sprang to action.

And after all, what need was there? wondered Joanna sadly. If Roger did not love Shuan yet, at least he must love what she would ultimately stand for in his mind—the age-old stability and continuance of Carrieghmere in which he had his roots and which would have its future in his children.

For little was more certain than that Roger Carnehill would marry, have children—and that she, Joanna, would not be there to see!

CHAPTER ELEVEN

Every day now Roger was beginning to be able to undertake the 'little more' which signified his body's return to strength and power. And increasingly every day Joanna expected to get the recall to London which would mark the ending of his case.

As the summer days drew on and the date of the Dublin Horse Show came nearer, Shuan and René Menden intensified their training of the mare, Lady of Belmont, which Shuan would ride in the chief Ladies' Jumping Event. Roger was able to turn out to watch them at the early morning practice, and often Joanna would go along too.

That summer the weather afforded some specially thorough examples of the Irish 'soft morning'—the fine, misting drizzle which drives up upon the south-west wind to blot out the horizon completely and to wet the unwary to the skin in a surprisingly short time. It was on one of these days that Joanna, deceived into thinking that the obscured sun would presently break through, had gone out without a coat.

She and Roger stood side by side, waiting for the other two to appear out of the mist for another round of the improvised course. Over his arm he was carrying Shuan's hooded camel-hair coat which she had discarded upon mounting, but it was not until Joanna gave an involuntary shiver that he seemed to be aware of the rain.

'Here, put this on,' he said quickly. 'What do you mean by invoking the elements in this way?'

'In England,' Joanna retorted, 'a misted morning sun usually means a fine day!'

'And in Eire even the sun takes its orders from the west wind!' He held the coat open, making an imperious gesture commanding her to put her arms into its sleeves. Joanna obediently turned her back and felt the coat's welcome warmth gradually drawn up on to her shoulders. But as she made to turn about, fumbling for the edge of the hood in order to draw it over her head, she found herself transfixed. Roger's hands were still at her shoulders, holding her fast.

For a moment Joanna's heart seemed to be throbbing in her very throat at the ecstasy of knowing his touch which had no relation to the thousand and one impersonal contacts they had had with each other and which for a blessed self-deceiving instant, she could believe to be an unspoken tribute of service from a man to a beloved woman...

But the moment passed. His hold slackened and she drew away, feeling again for the hood with fingers which trembled.

Their eyes met in an instant's unanswered question. Then he said lightly: 'In that thing you look about ten years old!'

'Do I—?' began Joanna, and then drew back quickly as Shuan and René on their mounts appeared suddenly from the veil of mist which was closing in upon them. Behind them, on foot, came Justin McKiley.

He and Roger greeted each other briefly. Then Roger turned to Shuan. 'How was it?' he asked. 'We couldn't see for the rain.'

'Not good enough. René had to fault me four times.'

'Where?'

'At a ditch and again at the gate. Roger, will you come over there with us and I'll try them again?'

'Of course.' He turned to Joanna. 'Will you come?'

She shook her head. 'No. I'll get back and see about organizing some hot coffee for you when you come in.'

She turned away, expecting Justin to accompany the others. Instead, he watched them move off and then fell into step beside her.

'I was coming up to the house anyway,' he explained easily. 'Shuan is a lovely little horsewoman, isn't she? I shouldn't be at all surprised to see her land a prize at Ballsbridge on the tenth.'

'If she does, it will be because she's worked for it, heart and soul,' declared Joanna.

'Yes, hasn't she?' he agreed smoothly. 'But of course I knew that's how it would be when we had to sell the other mare. Shuan is sufficiently Irish to regard a lost cause as something to be fought for to the death. When Deirdre went, she didn't believe Lady of Belmont had a chance of appearing at the Show, but that didn't stop her from setting her teeth into the idea of getting her there all the same. Haven't you found Shuan is like that—that she'll ride a conviction—however mistaken—to the last whiplash?'

'Yes, perhaps.' Joanna was not anxious to discuss Shuan's character with Justin, but he went on relentlessly:

'That's how I see it, and I know her pretty

172

well, I think. Besides, I find her an attractive child, and that's always an aid to the judging of character. Don't you agree?'

Joanna did not reply, and he went on mockingly:

'Come, *you* should know that I like to have attractive women about me. And since you made it clear that you had—other plans to pursue, how can you blame me for cultivating Shuan who is infinitely more—malleable?'

Joanna moistened her dry lips. 'Shuan says that you believe you can get her a job,' she said, finding it hard now to conceal her dislike of the man.

He looked surprised. 'Oh, did she tell you that?'

'She told Mrs. Carnehill when I happened to be there. She said you knew some influential people in the antique trade—'

'In *antiques*?' He laughed. 'Well, that was as good a story as any other, wasn't it?'

Joanna stared at him. The blatant admission confirmed Shuan's story. She said: 'You mean you never promised her anything of the sort?'

'Never in this world,' he retorted airily.

'Not even,' she asked with an uncontrollable touch of malice, 'the mysterious occupation which you once offered to me?'

The glance he gave her was a studied insolence. 'Not even that,' he said. 'On more sober thoughts I came to the conclusion that our friend Magda, for all her shortcomings, fulfils that particular role better than anyone else could. Besides, it suits *her*. A furnished flat in Merrion Square, clothes, money, good company—no, my sweet Magda would never forgive me if I offered *her* job to anyone else!'

'Then,' said Joanna breathlessly upon a sudden resolution, 'if the story that you were going to get Shuan a job was a complete fabrication, why do you trouble with her at all? She's years younger than you are, and—and she's in love with Roger Carnehill!'

Too late Joanna realized that in deciding to appeal to him for Shuan's sake she had betrayed to him—to him of all people!—the girl's secret.

They had reached the house now. With the merest gesture of a bow Justin made as if to leave her.

'That, my dear Joanna,' he said mockingly, 'would not surely be a consideration which you would expect to weight with *me*?'

Then he turned away in the direction of the stables and Joanna watched him go, wishing with all her heart that she had not counselled Roger to keep him on at Carrieghmere for a day longer than was necessary. The man was evil, she was convinced. But how he was seeking to use Shuan for his own ends, that she did not know.

When Horse Show Week came Dr. Beltane

advised Roger against trying to attend it.

'Next year, old chap, we'll probably all be there to see you competing. This year I'd give it a miss, if I were you, though of course you're not under my orders any longer.'

Roger accepted the advice with better grace than Joanna had expected. But this was typical of the new, adult person he had become since his recovery had set in—his petulant self-pity was a thing of the past. Shuan, however, was deeply disappointed and showed it, as a child would have done, in her crest-fallen face and trembling upper lip.

'Oh, Roger,' she said, 'I was *counting* on your being there!'

He took her by the shoulder and shook her gently. 'I'm sorry, poppet, but I know I couldn't stand the crowds. You'll have Mother and René to support you. Your event is bound to be on TV—Joanna and I will listen in and report back all the nice things the commentator says about you.'

Shuan turned to Joanna in surprise. 'Oh, aren't you coming either?'

'She'll be staying with me,' put in Roger quickly. It was a crisp, decisive statement of fact with which there was obviously to be no argument. He went on: 'How are you getting to Ballsbridge, by the way?'

'Major Petrie is letting me send Lady of Belmont over with his string,' Shuan told him. 'Mother and René are going with

Michael in the car, and—Justin has offered to take me.'

'And you've accepted the offer?'

'Yes, I—'

'Then I'd like you to tell him you've changed your plans, that you'll be going with the others.' Again it was clear that Roger was giving an order which was not to be questioned.

Shuan protested: 'But that's ridiculous! We shall be such a crowd, and Justin's car will be empty!'

'I'd still prefer that you didn't help to fill it,' retorted Roger coldly.

For a moment Shuan stared at him as if wondering whether to continue the argument. Then she shrugged her shoulders and turned away. But before she reached the door Roger said: 'Shuan!' His voice was unexpectedly gentle. 'Shuan, supposing Lady of Belmont were placed—what about a party of celebration?'

Her face lighted up instantly. 'Oh, Roger, how lovely! It would be the first since—well, for ages,' she substituted. 'But ought you to—I mean, could you stand it?'

'I'd try,' he promised with a smile. 'What form would you like it to take?'

'Oh, a dance—a fancy-dress affair with a band brought out from Dublin! Could—could we manage that, do you think? Roger darling, *could* we?'

'That,' he teased, 'is for Lady of Belmont to say!'

Her face fell slightly. 'Yes, of course. She must get a place. If only I were riding Deirdre—!'

But she went off happily enough, and Roger turned to Joanna with a grimace. 'Well—I'm committed!' he said.

'You made her very happy,' said Joanna quietly. 'I do hope her mare is placed.'

He looked at her indulgently. 'My dear Joanna, don't you realize that, even if Lady of Belmont took it upon herself to refuse at every jump on the course, I'm *still* committed to the dubious delights of a "fancy-dress affair with a band brought out from Dublin". It was that sort of a promise.' He frowned suddenly. 'In fact, it wasn't so much of a promise as—as a bribe! Though I haven't an idea why I should stoop to bribing her to keep away from the fellow!'

'She would not need bribery if you treated her more as an equal and less as a child to be alternately scolded and indulged!' Joanna heard herself saying almost sharply. 'She doesn't take orders graciously!'

After a moment she tried to give him a hint. She went on: 'I don't think, you know, that Shuan is actually attracted by Mr. McKiley. In fact, I don't know that she likes him at all.'

'Then why, in the name of goodness, does

she cultivate his company? She hasn't been doing it openly lately, but you can see for yourself that the association is still going on!'

'Yes, but—Well, from something Shuan said, I gathered that she had some reason of her own for it—a secret reason perhaps.'

Roger laughed a little cynically. 'If she imagined that she had, that would be just like her, though in Justin's case I can't think what it could be. But ever since she was a kid she has had periodic pursuits of cock-eyed ideas that she tries to turn into crusades, to which, while they're biting her, she is prepared to sacrifice herself and everyone else's peace of mind. But whatever her reason is this time, I'll get it out of her. I'll not tax her until she's free of this Horse Show business. But after that there'll be no more nonsense with McKiley. In any case, the whole thing will stop automatically, for McKiley goes at the end of the month.'

'Goes? You've decided that?'

'Yes.' He looked beyond her to the open park. 'He doesn't know it yet. But this—this half-light between my illness and my beginning to manage my own affairs must come to an end sometime. And it seems to me that the measure of it is my affair now. McKiley will go. And so, Joanna, must you.'

He was still not looking at her as she replied in a low voice: 'Yes. I am here still only under Dr. Beltane's orders. But I agree that it's for you to decide now. You don't need me any more.'

He looked back at her quickly. But her head was lowered and her eyes did not meet his. He said slowly: 'You must understand about this, Joanna. Justin's going will make me free of Carrieghmere again. But while you are here I can't belong completely to it. That's why you must go.'

'I do understand. You mean that I belong—as no one else about you does—to a time when your future with the estate seemed a very long way off? I think it's very natural that you should long to be rid of—of all the associations I stand for—'

'All the associations you stand for!' echoed Roger. 'Well, perhaps that's putting it as well as I could myself. But perhaps I have been tempted to put it more floridly by saying that you've been the blessed guide to my weaknesses, whereas I suppose I've got to find my strength—alone. I can't keep you for ever, Joanna. Don't you see that I'm afraid of finding that I've kept you too long?'

There was a strangely pleading note in his voice, a note which she did not understand. But she did not try to answer it. And she stilled the crying of her own heart with words which sounded as cold, as impersonal, but were as necessary as a surgeon's knife. She said:

'I do understand that you don't need to rely

179

upon me any longer—for anything. That's natural—and gratifyingly healthy. And we don't need to make an emotional issue of it, do we?'

*　　*　　*

After that, she noticed that Roger appeared to be at pains to emphasize the fact that he was no longer dependent on either her nursing or her company. He went out on to the estate every day now, and when it looked as if they might be left along together he would make an excuse to leave her or contrive for someone else to break up a possible *tête-à-tête*.

On the day of Shuan's ordeal at the Horse Show he was out all the morning, and when the time for the programme came around he asked Cook and Roseen to watch it too. And at an exciting point Mrs. Kimstone walked in, announcing herself brightly as having come to 'keep lonely Roger company'.

'The Colonel has gone to the Show, so I drove myself over, as I had heard you weren't going. Of course I didn't expect to find you surrounded by *bevies*—!' she said brightly, her eye lighting somewhat accusingly upon Joanna.

Roger ignored the archness of this remark as he motioned her to a seat and said briefly: 'Sit down and shut up, there's a good soul, Marty. The kid has had a clear round and she hasn't come on yet for the jump-off. But she's still got a chance of a place...'

With elaborate caution Mrs. Kimstone moved across to the chair he had indicated. 'I'll be like a little mouse,' she promised. 'Of course I realized how wrapped up you would be in watching Shuan's event. But I hadn't grasped that Nurse Merivale was still with you, or I wouldn't have made *rather* a sacrifice in coming over on what I *thought* was an errand of mercy—'

'Marty, *please*!' begged Roger.

The thin lips pursed and she looked slightly offended. 'Oh, all right,' she said. 'Now tell me, how far has Shuan got? But of course, you *were* just telling me, weren't you—?'

Her voice trailed away as Roger looked at her with renewed exasperation. And after that only the commentator's voice broke the silence.

Until at last—'... I'll repeat the result of that event. The winner was Agomar: Miss Hurry. The runner-up was Lady of Belmont: Miss Shuan Ferrall. The third place was taken by Random: Mrs. Clare Booset. We are now leaving the Dublin Horse Show at Ballsbridge and returning you to the studio...'

The little party relaxed its tension. Roger switched off and took a cigarette as if it had been something for which he had been waiting for a long time. He murmured: 'Second place! Good kid.' And that was all.

Joanna smiled across at him and said quietly: 'I'm awfully glad!' And Roseen, edging towards the door with Cook said: 'That makes Miss Shuan's party the certain thing now!'

Mrs. Kimstone, who had begun to say: 'Of course the *competition* nowadays is nothing to what it was—' pricked her ears with curiosity and demanded of Roger: 'Party? What party?'

'A fancy-dress dance I promised Shuan if she took a place at the Show. You'll be getting an invitation—'

'Fancy dress? Oh dear, that means the Colonel and I will have to be a Highland Lad and Lassie *again*! Couldn't you have made it a sober, decent affair of evening dress, Roger?'

'Not my idea. Shuan's entirely—' he was retorting cheerfully when the telephone began to ring.

Joanna rose to answer it, but he intervened. 'I'll go,' he said. 'It'll be Shuan, wanting to gloat.'

When he had gone Mrs. Kimstone took from her bag a piece of grey knitting which seemed identical with that on which she had been working months before. Frowning over it, she remarked: 'You know, I *didn't* expect to find you still here, Nurse. I'd understood that Roger was *completely* independent of care now—'

'Dr. Beltane wished me to stay on for a while. But I go very soon.'

'Before this party they have planned? What a pity!' Mrs. Kimstone's small eyes glittered.

'A pity?' Joanna did not think it necessary to say that the proposed date of the party was a week before that of her own departure from Carrieghmere.

'Well, yes. Because I daresay you would like to know that there was to be a happy ending for your patient. And I should think it likely that, now he is cured and can have complete confidence in his future, Roger will announce his engagement to Shuan at this party.'

'And I,' said Joanna quietly, 'should think it extremely improbable!'

Mrs. Kimstone looked at her sharply. 'Indeed, Nurse? Why? If I remember rightly, you took this attitude once before. Though how it ties up with that complete detachment you claim to preserve—!'

'It was you who suggested that I probably felt I ought to remain detached,' Joanna reminded her. 'Whereas I have—' she chose her words carefully, 'the—warmest interest in Mr. Carnehill's future. And I simply don't believe that he thinks—yet—of Shuan as his wife.'

'But she's devoted to him!'

'So we agreed before. But surely you don't suggest that Shuan herself would say that that

183

was—enough?'

'I don't know, I'm sure. But in my day,' retorted Mrs. Kimstone with asperity, 'a girl accepted an advantageous proposal of marriage without too much question. And Roger can offer her *everything!*'

'One day—I hope he may.' The brief words marked her heart's final renunciation. And once they were spoken she knew them to be true—she *did* hope that Roger would find fulfilment with Shuan, and not with some stranger whom she herself would never know.

'But you grudge him the possibility that he may *know* his own mind now! Really, Nurse, I think you exceed your office in presuming to predict your patient's future in this way!'

'Perhaps I do. I'm sorry,' said Joanna quietly, and controlled herself only with a difficulty as Mrs. Kimstone, ignoring the apology, went on with an assumed thoughtfulness:

'Of course there may be something more to it. You must have had quite a lot of influence with Roger while he's been ill, and that may have led you into mistaken notions of your own. You say you don't think he has the smallest notion of asking Shuan to marry him.' She frowned, as if in search of words with which to express her meaning. Then, triumphantly: 'Now you know, in my day we hadn't a word for that kind of thing. But don't these modern psychologists call it—*wishful thinking?*'

At which Joanna despised her caught breath which may have led Mrs. Kimstone to believe her shot had gone home.

CHAPTER TWELVE

For Shuan's dance Joanna thought of sending to London for a Cinderella costume which she had worn once at a nurses' social. But when she mentioned this to Mrs. Carnehill the older woman, with a perception which was unusual with her, said:

'You know, I can't quite see you as a Cinderella. You are so fair, so clean-cut. I always think of Cinderella—until that business with the pumpkin—as a mousy, insignificant creature. And no one could ever call you that, Joanna!'

'Well, does it matter?' asked Joanna with a smile that was a little weary.

'It does! I want you to shine at this party of ours. I wonder what else we could think of for you? Wait now, till I have it! Come with me.'

Obediently, Joanna followed the sturdy little figure out of the room and across to the long drawing-room which was so seldom used and where she had waited on the chill spring day for Dale Woodward to come to her for the last time.

On the far wall from the door hung the portrait of a girl at which she had looked vaguely on that day. Mrs. Carnehill halted before it.

Bewildered, Joanna stared. 'That's the Reynolds portrait,' she said obviously.

'Clarissa Carnehill,' supplemented the older woman gently. 'Roger's ancestress—English, as fair as you are, and painted by Sir Joshua Reynolds in 1767. Look at her now—hasn't she the look and figure of you to the very life?'

Joanna looked in silence. She saw a girl, seemingly of about her own age, dressed in the graceful high-waisted gown of the period and with a blue-lined cloak flung back from her shoulders. One long-fingered hand rested upon the head of an Irish wolfhound, the other was at her side, holding a wide-brimmed leghorn hat. Her skin was very fair and her hair was of the same pale gold as Joanna's own. Her eyes were blue where Joanna's were grey, but there was indeed in this girl of the eighteenth century, long since dead, a likeness to herself which she could not deny.

'What relation was she to—to you?' she asked Mrs. Carnehill.

'Nothing to me—except by marriage, of course. But she was Roger's great-great-great-grandmother. The Roger Carnehill of that day met her in London and married her before she was eighteen. I think she was about twenty-five when this portrait was painted. Your likeness to someone had puzzled me, but I knew who it was only when I was trying just now to picture you in the dress of some period not our own. Then I thought of Clarissa—and I knew that for you to *be* Clarissa at Shuan's party would be the only thing possible.'

'But I couldn't!' protested Joanna. 'The dress, for one thing—I couldn't hope to get that sprigged satin copied!'

'But I have it still!' said Mrs. Carnehill surprisingly.

'Not—not the dress itself?'

'Indeed I have. Not the hat, but the dress has always been kept carefully and is as good as it was then.'

'But I couldn't, Mrs. Carnehill,' repeated Joanna. In the first breathless moment she had used the difficulty of the dress as an excuse to cover the far deeper dismay she felt at the idea. She knew that she feared more than anything the scorn and anger Roger might show if she attempted to masquerade as his kinswoman.

'But it's only fun—a play—a kind of tableau!'

'All the same, I can't think that Mr. Carnehill would—would care for it,' murmured Joanna wretchedly.

'Roger? He'll not be told anything about it

until he sees you at the dance! You'd have to promise that you wouldn't tell him. It's my idea entirely and it's to be my secret. And what objection would he have, to be sure?'

'Well, don't you see that the picture, even the dress itself, must have associations for your family on which I haven't any right to intrude? There must be someone close to him for whom the dress should be kept. Shuan—'

'Shuan?' Mrs. Carnehill looked up at the portrait critically. 'Tell me now,' she countered, 'have you ever seen Shuan with the look of *that* girl upon her? And there's the difference in their colouring—Shuan, with the wild Irish darkness of her, and Clarissa, open and fair. No, the fancy I have to see a living Clarissa at the dance would be lost entirely if Shuan attempted it. Come now, Joanna, say you'll indulge me!'

'I'd love to.'

'Then that's settled. You are doing it to please me. Come upstairs with me now, and I'll show you the dress and the cloak this minute.'

*   *   *

A day or two before the dance Shuan asked abruptly: 'What are you coming as?'

'A secret!' hedged Joanna smilingly.

'That's all right, I only asked. I didn't suppose you'd tell me,' returned Shuan

188

imperturbably. Then with an oblique look she went on: 'I've asked Justin to the dance. Do you suppose Roger is going to mind?'

'I shouldn't think so. It would have been difficult *not* to invite him, wouldn't it?'

'Yes. So he's coming. He's bringing Magda too.'

'Oh. Neither Mrs. Carnehill nor Mr. Carnehill have met her, have they?'

'What you mean is—they won't like her!' said Shuan in quick defiance.

'Do *you* like her?' queried Joanna.

Shuan shrugged. 'She's all right,' she said again, adding naïvely: 'I enjoy—just looking at her.'

Joanna agreed. 'She is rather—exquisite, isn't she?'

Shuan nodded. 'Yes. Her clothes—! You know, she must have an awful lot of money, though she doesn't work, and she doesn't seem to have any people.'

Joanna bent her head over the fine linen cloth which she was darning for Mrs. Carnehill. 'I think,' she said carefully, 'that, from something he said to me, Mr. McKiley—helps her.'

'You mean that she does some sort of job for him?'

'Yes—perhaps—' (How could she express to Shuan her own idea of the undefined relationship between Magda and Justin McKiley of which her knowledge of the man had warned her?)

She was not prepared for the girl's reception of her hesitating admission. There was neither embarrassment nor reserve in Shuan's retort: 'But that's not news! I've known *that* for a long time!'

Joanna looked up quickly. 'What do you mean?' she demanded.

'Well, that Magda does some sort of job for Justin and that he pays her well for it. When I said about her having plenty of money and not having any people or anything I wanted to know if you'd guessed too—'

'I didn't have to. He told me.'

'He didn't tell you what she *does*?'

'No.' A wave of misgiving, even of fear, flooded over Joanna. She remembered suddenly that which both Justin and Roger had said of Shuan. Justin had said: 'She will ride a conviction to the last whiplash.' And Roger: 'She has periodic pursuits of cock-eyed ideas to which she is prepared to sacrifice herself and everyone else's peace of mind.' And it seemed to Joanna that she herself might have stumbled unawares upon some secret mission which, however misguided, just now appeared to Shuan as the very meaning of her life.

She said urgently: 'Shuan, what are you hinting at? You're making a mystery of something! What do you *know*?'

'I *don't* know! I'm guessing too—!'

190

There was an airy note in her voice which touched Joanna jarringly. She said sharply: 'Well, don't—I beg of you—interfere in something you don't understand. If there's anything about Justin McKiley or Magda or the two of them that you can only guess at, leave it alone. I believe I know the man better than you possibly could. *And you can't but get hurt* if you try to—to meet him on his own ground.'

Shuan laughed. 'Hurt? How could I get hurt? Justin is nothing to me! And people don't get hurt unless they care about somebody else—too much. And I don't even particularly *like* Justin. Ask René—he knows what I felt about Justin's selling Deirdre when I don't believe he need have done. So it's impossible that he could have any power to hurt me. And I—happen to be enjoying myself immensely!'

Joanna made one last effort. 'Shuan, if you won't tell me what all this is about, will you tell—Roger, before it's too late?'

'Roger? Least of all Roger! And *you're* not to tell him anything!'

Joanna sighed. 'There's nothing I could tell him,' she said wearily. 'And it seems that there's nothing I can say to you either. Except to warn you that, whatever particular form of fire you're playing with, remember that it could burn Roger too!'

Without a word Shuan turned away, and it

191

seemed to Joanna that for all her liking of the girl, for all the poignancy of their love for the same man, the curtain of alien hostility between them was as impenetrable as ever.

★   ★   ★

The girl's spirits seemed unaffected, but Joanna was still depressed by the encounter when she found herself caught up in the more cheerful mysteries attending the last preparations for the dance.

On the evening itself Mrs. Carnehill drew her aside to whisper: 'The dress and the cloak, and the hat I managed to get for you in Dublin, are laid out on your bed. I put them there myself. Then I locked the door—here is the key.' She dropped it into Joanna's hand and went on: 'You'll dress early, won't you? Because I want to smuggle you into the drawing-room and the timing is going to be difficult. I *don't* want Roger to see you first—that would spoil everything. So I want to have him and Shuan occupied in greeting some of the first-comers while I manage to get you in through the french windows. We'll probably have to hang about on the terrace for a bit. What a mercy that it's a warm night!'

Joanna laughed. 'You treat me as if I were a special kind of tableau that must be organized and arranged in secret!'

'Well, that's my idea. That's why I've

borrowed a wolfhound for you. Anyway I don't expect you to trail him around all the evening, but I *do* want the representation of the portrait to be complete, if only for as long as you can hold the pose. You'll do it to please me, won't you, Joanna?'

'Of course!'

'Good girl. You see, it'll be a diversion—something to set people talking, to warm them up. Run along and dress now. I'll come and help you with your hair, and then we'll watch our moment for slipping out on to the terrace.'

Not knowing whether she did it reluctantly or eagerly, Joanna went up to her room. There lay the dress and the cloak which had belonged to Clarissa Carnehill, but for a long time after she was ready to do so she did not put them on. She was thinking: 'I mustn't let this mean more than it really does. It's only fun, after all, and Mrs. Carnehill is so fascinated with the idea that I've simply *got* to play up ... But oh, I can't *help* its meaning something more to me! By this night's work I am only tying another knot in the rope of association and memory that binds me to this place—and to the thought of Roger. I haven't been brave enough to cut myself free before I must—and the slow fraying of the rope is going to take so long—'

And it was so that Mrs. Carnehill found her. 'Joanna, child, you've been dawdling!'

she scolded. 'People are beginning to arrive and Roger is giving them drinks. We've got about a quarter of an hour—'

She checked as Joanna turned about, her face white and her lips trembling a little.

'I—can't,' she whispered. 'I—don't *belong*—!'

For a moment Mrs. Carnehill's gaze was very steady. Then without a word she lifted the dress from the bed, held it out in readiness for Joanna to put on. 'It will be all right,' she promised. 'And you are doing it for me.'

Joanna said nothing, and when she had slipped her housecoat over the low-cut bodice of the dress they both worked upon the arrangement of her hair.

In faithful imitation of the portrait, they parted it down the centre, then with the help of combs looped it in two forward sweeping 'wings' at each side. Then, since nothing would induce its fineness into the appropriate series of ringlets for the rest of it, Mrs. Carnehill brushed and turned it under so that its length was concealed in a thick 'page-boy' sweep upon Joanna's neck. She tied on the cloak by its broad ribbons which were faded but very soft, and put the hat into the girl's hand. Then she stood back to survey her handiwork.

'Not Joanna Merivale any longer—Mistress Clarissa Carnehill to the life!' she said

194

triumphantly.

On the terrace in the dusk Michael was waiting for them, with the borrowed wolfhound straining upon a leash.

A few minutes later Joanna was posed—a little to the left of the Reynolds portrait—to Mrs. Carnehill's satisfaction. She and Michael stood back admiringly and she was murmuring: 'It's—perfect, Joanna!' when voices were heard outside the door, and a press of ten or a dozen people came in.

Roger was there, talking to a girl in a white froth of columbine fluffiness—Roger, tall, upright, his red hair aflame above a short-tunicked costume of green leather, his legs bound about with thongs, and a green-lined cloak fastened upon one shoulder by a great embossed clasp. The cloak reached the floor and lay in a swirl about his feet as, halfway across the room, he saw Joanna and stood transfixed.

For a moment it seemed to Joanna that they were alone ... That, for all the chatter and movement about them, they had achieved with each other a kind of desert of intimacy where, she could imagine, many an unsaid thing passed between them.

But with nonchalance, with an air, she held her pose. One hand rested upon the head of the wolfhound, the other held the leghorn hat at her side. Her head was high and about her lips played the little calm smile of the girl in

195

the portrait.

Someone—a woman—exclaimed: 'What a super idea! *Too* enchanting!'

The spell broke. The twentieth century was about them again. But Roger stepped forward to lift, with a slightly mocking gesture, Joanna's fingers to his lips.

He said: 'King Conchubor greets a lady of Ireland who came long after his time—a matter for his profoundest regret!'

And Joanna, accepted her cue, dropped a straight-backed little curtsey as she replied: 'The regret, sire, is mutual!'

Everyone laughed and glancing at Mrs. Carnehill, Joanna noticed that she looked gratified with the result of her plot. Roger glanced at his mother, too, and said mock-reprovingly: 'Mother—you're not properly dressed!'

Mrs. Carnehill looked apologetically at the befrilled and figured satin of her evening gown. Her voice was slightly pathetic as she said: 'Oh, Roger, I'm too old for this sort of thing! I don't have to be a post office *again*, do I?'

There was another concerted laugh, as if everyone understood the joke. Roger turned to Joanna. 'Mother's perennial fancy dress is a pillar-box. But now, apparently, she is contracting out of public service.'

At that moment there was another surge of movement at the door. A fresh group of people came in. Among them were Shuan, Justin McKiley, and Magda. René was there too—dressed as a sixteenth-century Lowland soldier.

At sight of Shuan, Joanna barely suppressed a gasp. How lovely the girl was! Her costume was so completely right for her colouring and her personality that it seemed that all the latent taste which did not go to her everyday dressing had gone to the choice of it.

Her dark hair hung loosely about her shoulders from which hung a mist of grey-green draperies which were bound about her waist with a thick silver rope and hung in an uneven, diaphanous line above her ankles. Her feet were bare. Somehow she wasn't Shuan any more—she was eternally faerie...

'Who is she? murmured Joanna.

'Etain, I think,' said Roger. 'Etain, who gave up her fairyhood in order to marry the man she loved.' He paused. 'The fairies claimed her again, of course. I've often wondered how willing she was to go...'

His glance passed from Shuan to the people she was with. Justin McKiley, Joanna noticed, was blatantly and arrogantly modern in faultless evening clothes. So was Magda, in a beautifully modelled gown of white silk shot with gold. In her ears she wore heavy 'gipsy' ear-rings of gold to match the broad bangles at her wrist. The effect was striking and exotic, but not, Joanna felt, in the best of taste at a party at which the other guests had carried out their hostess' wish by accepting the doubtful comfort of 'fancy dress'.

Shuan was bringing them over to Roger and Mrs. Carnehill in order to introduce Magda, and Joanna stood aside. But she was near enough to notice the formality of Roger's greeting to Magda, even the slight frown between his eyes which she had come to know so well. He was annoyed.

The twentieth century flowed insistently in again ... The 'band from Dublin' struck up, the groups shifted, became reassorted, and the first few people began to dance.

Justin McKiley bowed to Shuan and they moved off together. Joanna believed that Roger would invite Magda, but, explaining formally that he would be dancing very little, he introduced her to a stranger at the same moment as Joanna was claimed by Colonel Kimstone.

Beyond that first piece of mocking play-acting Roger had not spoken to her.

It was a little later when, making conversation with a shy youth who had been her last partner, her attention was taken by some talk going on nearby.

A woman whom she did not know was saying: 'Rather off, I thought.' And then a voice which she recognized said in a little insinuating half-whisper: 'Well, so did I. I

198

mean, his own ancestress and she, a nurse out from England for a few months! It isn't as if she was anyone the Carnehills actually *knew*—in the ordinary way, I mean! And using the very gown itself, I understand from his mother. When she told me, I said, "Edna, what effrontery of her to suggest it!" And all Edna said was: "She didn't. *I* did!"'

Deliberately Joanna leaned towards her partner. 'You were saying—?' she urged.

But the conversation she did not want to overhear came through ... Mrs. Kimstone's companion remarked with relish: 'Well, Roger at least didn't know anything about it. Completely taken aback, *I* thought!'

'As surprised as he was annoyed, I should say. After all, if anyone should be allowed to play-act in Carnehill heirlooms it should be Shuan, not an English miss who hasn't a—'

Flushed and annoyed with herself as much as with the two gossiping women, Joanna stood up abruptly. She had to get away, *had* to—!

When she came back into the drawing-room another dance was in full swing. She stood watching, noticing idly that Shuan was dancing again with Justin McKiley ...

A voice at her shoulder said quietly: 'May I find you a partner?' It was Roger, his voice as formal as if they were almost complete strangers.

'Don't bother, please. This dance must be half over—'

'Yes.' There was a pause. Then: 'May I, for the rest of it, have the privilege? I'm not dancing, of course. Would you find it warm enough out on the terrace?'

'Yes, I think so—'

He turned and, side by side, they went out on to the stone terrace where chairs had been placed, but which was quite deserted.

Joanna sat down near the low parapet, Roger leaned against it, facing her, his arms folded.

He said: 'I hope you're going to agree with me that I might have been consulted!'

Joanna looked up quickly. But she could distinguish only his profile in the darkness.

'I'm sorry,' she said. 'I didn't think it was suitable and that you might be very reasonably annoyed. But Mrs. Carnehill particularly asked me not to tell you.'

'*Mother* did? You mean that she *was* consulted by Shuan, and that she was against my being told?'

'Shuan—?' Joanna's voice was hesitant, puzzled.

Roger leaned forward in order to look into her upturned face. 'Are we at cross-purposes?' he asked quietly. 'I'm inclined to think we're not talking about the same things.'

'I don't know. Don't you mean that you

think my appearing as a copy of the Reynolds portrait was in bad taste and that you should have been told about it?' asked Joanna wretchedly.

There was a little pause. Then Roger laughed, though not very mirthfully.

He asked: 'How could you think I minded about that?'

'Don't you? I thought you might. I'm—not one of your family—'

'Neither,' he pointed out dryly, 'was Clarissa—until she married into it. She was English, as you are—'

'Yes.' Joanna made a desperate effort to tell herself that she was relieved that he had not taken her masquerade in the wrong spirit. But she found his indifference as painful as his anger. She steadied herself in order to say: 'So we were at cross-purposes. *You* were talking about something to do with Shuan?'

'Yes, of course. I want to know how she had the presumption to ask McKiley and that—that woman to this affair—to this house?'

'But how could she *not* ask Mr. McKiley?' asked Joanna in surprise. 'While he's still here, presumably he's accepted by your friends?' (As *I* am not by some of them! she though in bitter parenthesis.)

'Well, perhaps he had to come.' Roger conceded the point grudgingly. 'But the woman Magda—I suppose she invited

201

herself?' he added sarcastically.

'I don't know. But Shuan asked me if I thought you would mind if she asked Mr. McKiley, and told me at the same time that Magda would be coming too—'

'She consulted you? And you took it upon yourself to guarantee my complacence?

'You know my opinion of McKiley. You know I've always distrusted him, though perhaps you don't know that I've learnt a good deal more about him lately. I know that he's dined here before now at Mother's invitation, though mostly when I insisted on talking business with him. And I realize that you yourself have accepted his hospitality'— Joanna winced—'but how Shuan could imagine that I would countenance his bringing Magda here—!'

Astonishingly, and against her will Joanna found herself forced into a defence of Justin McKiley. 'I fail to see,' she said coldly, 'how he could avoid it if Shuan asked her.'

'And if you had assured Shuan that I couldn't possibly mind!'

Joanna moistened her dry lips. 'When Shuan spoke to me I gathered that it was settled they should come. I had no idea that she was saying nothing to you. Even if I had—'

'Yes? Even if you had?'

'Well, there mightn't have seemed anything wrong. I understand that Magda is employed by Mr. McKiley in some capacity.'

'And you accept that at its face value?'

'For want of any proof to the contrary, I must.'

Again Roger laughed, but it was not a pleasant sound. 'I'm afraid my innocence isn't of that crystal clarity,' he said shortly. 'Quite apart from the fact that McKiley happens to be employed by me, and has no right to delegate authority to anyone else! I'll only say that I should have preferred that neither Mother, nor Shuan—nor you, Joanna— should have to accept a questionable relationship of that sort in *this* house—*mine*!'

Suddenly the indignation Joanna had called to her own defence seemed to fade away. She knew only a kind of pity for Roger—an understanding of the hurt pride of family and of code which had spoken in his voice.

She said gently: 'If I had guessed you would care so much I would have discussed it with you. But'—she hesitated—'it hasn't been easy to talk to you lately.'

Roger said: 'It hasn't been easy to talk to you either. I hoped you might understand when I tried to tell you why you must go.'

'I did understand!' It was almost a cry.

Roger looked at her, a long look in the merciful darkness. 'Did you?' he said. 'I wonder!'

★   ★   ★

In the drawing-room behind them the dance had ended and had been followed by a wild Irish round dance involving nearly everyone. It ended with a burst of music of tarantella speed; the men spread their arms to trap the girls as they sped past; Shuan, caught, found that she must choose between René and Justin McKiley.

She hesitated. Then, with a look which the older man found provocative, she danced away with René.

'Too bad!' drawled Magda behind him as the music stopped. She, too, had joined in the dance, but she was as cool and unruffled as a newly blown lily.

His only reply was to motion her towards the open french windows. They passed through them on to the terrace just as Joanna and Roger left it.

CHAPTER THIRTEEN

The inevitable air of lassitude of the 'morning after' descended upon Carrieghmere next day. At breakfast Mrs. Carnehill announced that, though she was bone-tired, she must go to Dublin. Roger, after bidding her goodbye and joking with her about her work as he would never have done earlier, disappeared out on to the estate, and Shuan, coming late to the table in a tweed suit which effectually dispelled the memory of the ethereal Shuan of the previous night, was brief and non-committal in her conversation. Then she, too, went out, and Joanna, with her flight to England only a few days ahead, went to her room in order to begin her packing.

As she worked she was wondering whether by now she was perhaps glad to go ... What, after all, had she hoped for from that brief excursion into the personality and the clothes of the dead Clarissa Carnehill who had *belonged* here as she could never hope to?

The telephone rang, interrupting her thoughts. And a few minutes later Roseen came to her room.

'You heard the phone, maybe? 'Twas Mr. Roger, to say he wouldn't be back for lunch. You'll be in yourself, Nurse?'

'Yes. But don't bother about much for me—'

Roseen lingered at the door. 'Sure, we'll be missing you when you're gone,' she said.

Joanna looked up and smiled. 'I shall miss all of you, too. Tell me, have you thought any more of taking up nursing yourself?'

Roseen fidgeted with her apron. 'Well, I have, so. And I haven't, if you know what I mean.'

'Is it your mother who is the difficulty still?'

'Arrah, it is not. Isn't herself at me, all the time now, to be gone? For she says—what do you think?—that Michael couldn't keep me! And him with his stable apprenticeship behind him these three years, and knowing all he does be knowing about cars!'

'Are you engaged to Michael?' asked Joanna gently.

Roseen looked evasively ceilingwards. 'He has asked me. But I haven't said I will or I won't. Tell me now'—she fixed Joanna with an earnest eye—'do you think it is a good thing that a husband and wife would be at quarrelling all the while?'

'*All* the while? And about big things—or little ones?'

'Little ones, mostly. And maybe not all the while. With Michael there'd be some strange, sweet times—And sometimes, when I think of any other girl getting him in my place I know I'd be wanting to scratch out the eyes of her. That'd be a good test that'd prove I really love him, wouldn't it?' she added hopefully.

Joanna hesitated. 'It could be one, Roseen,' she said slowly. 'But I don't know that it could be the best. You see, I think that if you love someone very much you want for them whatever *they* want. Or at least, whatever you believe would make them most happy. It could be that you could even bring yourself to—to give them up for that reason.'

206

'You mean—if there was another girl after Michael I'd have to give him up?'

Joanna shook her head. 'Only if that was the way Michael wanted it. Or if you believed that he would find more happiness with her than with you. It'd be an awfully difficult decision to make, I know—'

'And supposing I came to deciding that way, what would become of *me*?' asked Roseen blankly.

'Well, you'd be the one who would go on alone. You'd have to tell yourself'—Joanna spoke slowly, looking into her own future rather than into Roseen's—'that another door—a door to a different kind of happiness—would open for you one day. You'd *have* to hope that or—you wouldn't be able to go on.'

For a moment there was silence. Then Roseen said simply: 'But Michael doesn't want any other girl. He wants me!'

Joanna smiled. 'In that case, this is what might be described as a purely academic discussion, isn't it?' Then, as Roseen looked puzzled, she added. 'I mean, I expect you've already made up your mind to marry Michael, haven't you?'

Roseen blushed. 'Maybe I have. But maybe I won't be telling himself that—yet!'

She went away then, returning rather breathlessly a minute or so later to ask Joanna to come to speak to 'Mr. Menden, the French gentlemen, who's in the hall now, in a great tear to see Mr. Roger or the mistress. Something about Miss Shuan—'

Joanna's heart seemed to turn over. Had that vague 'something' which she had feared might be lying in wait for Shuan caught up with the girl—with all of them—at last?

René was not waiting patiently in the hall. He was pacing up and down, his apprehension written all over his pale, set face. In silence he followed Joanna into Mrs. Carnehill's study and faced her as she shut the door.

'Monsieur Carnehill—they tell me he is not here?'

'No. He has just left a message to say that he won't be in to lunch.'

She believed that René looked almost relieved at her reply. But he went on: 'And Madame Carnehill?'

'She had to go to Dublin. What is it, René? Roseen said it was something about Shuan—She—she's not hurt or anything?'

'*Mon Dieu*, not that!' he breathed. 'But something has happened. I must tell you—'

'Go on—'

'*Eh bien*, it was an hour ago—perhaps more—that Shuan has come down to the Dower House and soon has driven away with Mr. McKiley in his car—'

'They went quite openly?' put in Joanna.

'Oh, they make no secret of it. Me, I am

208

hurt—*here*'—René laid an expressive hand over his heart—'but I think nothing of it. Recently it has been often so. But when they have been gone some time the telephone rings and it is Magda, saying Justin McKiley has taken Shuan to keep a rendezvous with two men at Musveen, on the border of Eire and Northern Ireland. But it is no friendly meeting, you understand. For these men are of the underworld; they make *le contrebande*. They—' René sought the word—'smuggle drugs which are brought in by air through Shannon and passed by Justin, helped by Magda, to agents who carry them across the border or over to England. When Justin is not free to keep the rendezvous, Magda takes his place. But always it is different. Today Musveen. The next time somewhere else—'

Joanna gasped, feeling that the implications of this news were too vast to take in all at once. She said in bewilderment: 'You mean—Magda was *betraying* Justin McKiley? Betraying him to you?'

'She has done more than that. Before she has telephoned to me she has told the police of the rendezvous at Musveen. She has said that perhaps they do not believe she tells the truth over the telephone. *Naturellement*, she has not given them her name ... But she knows that they will risk nothing—the police will be at Musveen too.'

'And Shuan has gone with him? Could

209

Magda know that?'

René nodded. 'Mr. McKiley has told her that he would take Shuan with him. Last night—I think—they have quarrelled. And Magda, who for a long time has been the liaison, you understand, between him and the people with whom he must do business, has refused to go to Musveen with him. He has told her that he will take Shuan instead. So, for hate and jealousy of Shuan, she has betrayed them both. I think'—René's voice was bitter—'that Magda has enjoyed her conversations at the telephone this morning. And me—because I must hear and understand all that she has to tell me—must listen instead of going to her, taking her throat between my hands and *strangling* her!'

'But what did you mean,' protested Joanna, 'betrayed them both? Shuan is absolutely innocent! She can't know anything of the purpose of this journey!'

'Magda has said something more,' said René quietly. 'She has said that she told the police that there are to be four people at the rendezvous—the two men, McKiley and—a woman. A woman who has been acting as liaison between the parties for months. And, you understand, there will be a woman there—*Shuan*!'

'But she knows nothing!' repeated Joanna wildly.

'That will have to be proved. There cannot

210

but be a—sullying of her name, if no worse,' replied René gravely.

She said urgently: 'What can we do? Can we follow them? Warn her?'

René said: 'We must do that—even if we may not be in time. The car?'

'Michael drove Mrs. Carnehill to Tulleen station in it. But he'll be back by now. I'll find him—' She turned to the door, then stopped. 'René—McKiley's Lincoln!—how *can* we hope to equal the speed he can get out of that?'

René's lips set grimly. 'He is ahead of us by perhaps an hour and a half—but he may not hurry. We shall. And if anyone can overtake him, Michael can!'

Joanna nodded, a little comforted. She remembered that night journey back from Dublin when the Carrieghmere car had travelled as if on wings beneath Michael's hands.

At his suggestion René then went to fetch Michael while she hunted up road maps and wondered what message she ought to leave for Roger.

She was still struggling with this when René came back.

'Leave nothing,' he advised. 'What is it possible to tell him, after all?'

Joanna doubted the wisdom of this, but there was no time for argument. René said: 'Are you ready?' And she knew that she was

211

glad that neither in his mind nor in hers was there any question that they should not go together to Shuan's aid.

★   ★   ★

The long road stretched before them like a white ribbon. Joanna sat alone in the back seat; René, the map open on his knees, directed Michael without check. Apart from this, no one spoke.

As the miles slipped by Joanna had time to think, though for the most part her thoughts were a jigsaw pattern of bewilderment, lacking coherence.

She remembered again Roger's criticism of Shuan. How right he had been when he had said that, for the sake of pursuing a single-minded channel of her own, she cared little for the peace of mind of those about her—people she claimed to love! How far, Joanna wondered, had she become involved with Justin and his shady activities? And why, *why* had she ever dared to meddle with them in the first place?

For Joanna believed that she understood matters so far. Somehow, Shuan had stumbled upon the truth—though probably only upon half the truth—of Justin's dealings in this filthy illicit traffic. Justin himself had possibly given her the first boasting hint. For, looking back now, Joanna realized that

Justin, secure in his almost undisputed authority at Carrieghmere during Roger's illness, had barely attempted to conceal the fact that he had other sources of income than his pay.

The luxury of his car, the bizarre modernity of his part of the Dower House, even his shameless boast that Magda was dependent on him for her own luxuries—everything went to show that he had few qualms that he might be found out.

He had boasted to Joanna—why not to Shuan also? But it was strange that it had taken Shuan's inexperience to follow his complacent hints to some kind of conclusion! Roger had always distrusted the man, as she, Joanna, had done later. And Mrs. Carnehill, long before she had voiced her fears either to Joanna or to her son, had known that there was something deeply wrong at Carrieghmere. But Shuan alone had acted—however disastrously!

Poor Shuan! Why had she done it? For the hatred of Justin McKiley which René had suspected? Or for the love of, and in service of, Roger himself? What, supposing she did gain irrefutable evidence against Justin, did she intend to do with her facts? And had she ever considered the possibility of what had happened now—that she herself might be caught up in the amateurish web she had prepared for her victim?

. . . Leitrim . . . Balieborough . . . Drumkerry—the little towns along the road began with a scatter of cottages, quickened into life in a broad market-place fed by cross-roads, and became things of the past as the last animal inhabitant of each scurried from the path of the speeding car.

René said: 'We ought, I think, to find out if the Lincoln has been seen.'

'Oh, don't stop,' urged Joanna. 'Surely every minute is precious if we're to catch them before they reach Musveen?'

'Yes. But it would encourage us—no?—if we could learn certainly that they are in front—that we are upon the right road. So much is possible—'

Joanna's heart sank. So much was indeed possible—even that this journey was a hare-brained scheme doomed to failure. Resignedly she agreed. 'All right. Will you stop somewhere and ask? I suppose the chances that they have, or have not been seen, are about even.'

'The Lincoln—it is a car *d'élégance*,' said René shrewdly. 'It is more than possible that someone has noticed it and envied its owner.' He looked at his watch. 'Perhaps they have even stayed somewhere for a drink or perhaps for lunch. At the next town we will ask.'

At their first inquiry they drew blank. No one had noticed the Lincoln. But at the next village they learned that it has passed through more than an hour earlier.

'An hour!' Joanna said in dismay. 'That means we've gained very little! Have we any hope, René?'

He looked grave, but he said staunchly: 'For them there is no need to hurry. And I think that somewhere they will have stayed to take lunch. At Ballyboy, perhaps ... It is—how do you say—a landmark on the route and more than half-way. We will ask again at Ballyboy.'

In the town they drew up outside the only hotel which René thought McKiley would have been likely to visit. Michael went into the car-park at the side to inquire about the Lincoln, and René alighted too. He stood by the open door of the car and, looking at Joanna, he said with a half-smile:'The little Shuan—gives much trouble, does she not?'

'Yes. The worst of it is that she could never have meant to. She must have believed that she was doing something big for Mr. Carnehill—for Carrieghmere itself, perhaps—by following up some suspicions she had of Mr. McKiley. That's how it seems to me.'

'To me also. She is brave—and so very, very foolish!' There was no censure in René's voice—only a great tenderness.

'For you—it doesn't matter that for the purpose of this ill-conceived scheme of hers she has cultivated McKiley's attentions for weeks, that she has set out unescorted on this trip with him, that she is liable even now to find herself—and all of you—mixed up with the police?' asked Joanna impulsively.

'But for me—none of it matters. Me, I could not mind if we did not overtake her until she reaches Musveen—except for the shock which awaits her there and the shame involved for her guardian, for Mr. Carnehill. You see, I love her.'

At that moment Michael came back, got into his seat, and switched on the engine. They had moved off before he said: 'There's a fella in the yard says the Lincoln was parked there for over half an hour, an' a man an' a girl drove off north in her about twenty minutes back!'

'Twenty minutes! That is better!' commented René with satisfaction. Joanna said nothing. She, too, had felt the grip of a hope that there was a good chance now of their overtaking the Lincoln.

Beyond Ballyboy the road ran on levelly towards Monaghan, the next town ahead. But they were destined not to reach it...

On each side of the road were broad verges of stiff, reedy grass upon which errant donkeys, seemingly far from home, were to be seen grazing rather hopelessly. And it was upon one such stretch that they came upon the parked Lincoln.

Michael, uttering an exclamation at which

Joanna thought fleetingly she should have been shocked and wasn't, brought their own car with a shudder of brakes to a halt behind it. Rene already had the door open on his side. He got out. Joanna followed. But for whatever 'rescue' of Shuan they had planned they were too late. Shuan was already in the act of rescuing herself.

As they reached the other car she stumbled out of the near door, panting and half-sobbing. She seemed bewildered, and at sight of Joanna she stared unbelievingly.

Then she looked at René. With a gesture that was as simple and as unaffected as that of a father welcoming a tired child home he opened his arms to her.

She ran to him and he held her close, cradling her head upon his shoulder. And Joanna had scarcely time to wonder or to question the utter naturalness of it all before she heard Shuan murmuring brokenly: 'René, I'm so terribly, terribly sorry! How did you know? *How did you know?*'

'Later, *chérie*—later!' he whispered. 'First, we must take you home!'

But by now Justin McKiley had alighted and was leaning against the hood of the Lincoln with an unpleasant smile upon his face.

He bowed elaborately in René's direction. 'An extremely touching piece of knight-errantry!' he sneered. 'Though believe it or

217

not, you are very welcome to my late victim. I was just on the point of throwing her out—'

Shuan's head came up sharply as she twisted about in René's hold.

'That's a lie!' she declared. 'I *made* you stop the car. I—I threatened to jump if you didn't!'

Justin shrugged his shoulders insolently. 'A quibble, I think! Shall we agree that we are each glad to be free of the other's company? You'll excuse me, perhaps?'

This time his bow was for Joanna. But it was René who sprang forward to take him roughly by the shoulder.

'*Cochon!*' he said. 'I have waited for this!' His right fist came up in a blow directed at the other man's jaw, but he twisted adroitly at the right moment and stepped backward.

'You will not fight?' demanded René incredulously.

'I don't fight—schoolboys!'

'Ah-h!' René's furious lunge promised to be dangerous. But Shuan ran forward to catch him by the arm. 'René, don't! It was as much my fault as his. Let him go. I'll explain everything!'

The interruption was all that Justin needed in order to extricate himself from the situation. He turned towards his car, but as he made to get into it Joanna took an impulsive step forward. 'Don't go on—!' she said urgently.

He was seated now, one hand upon the wheel, the other upon the switch.

'Don't go on—where?' he asked.

'To—to Musveen—or wherever you were going!'

He raised his eyebrows. 'So you knew that? But of course, you had to, or you wouldn't have organized the rescue-party! And you could have known it from only one source. Well, well, I must say that my sweet Magda throws a pretty revenge—!'

'She's done more than that—*listen*—!'

But the urgency in Joanna's voice was drowned beneath the throbbing hum of the Lincoln's engine as Justin switched on. She was forced to step aside quickly as the car rocked across the reedy stubble, accelerated amazingly, and was gone.

She turned back to the others, making a gesture that was eloquent of helplessness as she did so.

'We should have *made* him listen!' she declared.

But René said: 'Let him go. It is a reward that he has asked for. There is nothing we can do.'

Joanna doubted that, but it was after all, Shuan, not Justin, whom they had come all this way to protect; Shuan for whom lay in front the inevitability of questions, the ordeal of judgment . . .

Soberly the car took the road along which

they had come. Michael was driving more steadily now. He and Joanna made a few perfunctory remarks to each other, but it seemed that all were occupied with their own thoughts. Until suddenly Shuan said urgently: 'I—I don't want to go home yet—until I've explained. Can't we stop somewhere? I—want to talk!'

It was with a sort of innate delicacy that Michael took the hint that she meant she wanted to talk to René and Joanna alone. He growled: 'I have an uncle lives two or three miles ahead. Maybe I could be let t' go t' see me uncle, the way ye'd be givin' Miss Shuan a drop t' warm her at the hotel?'

The 'hotel' in question proved to be the general shop-cum-public-house-cum-post office which covers under one roof all the legitimate needs of many a small Irish village.

In a bar-parlour that was chilly with leatherette and oilcloth, Joanna, Shuan and René faced each other across the gentle slope of the round table which had for decoration a celery glass full of plaited reeds tortured into fantastic shapes.

Joanna was glad to accept a cigarette from René, but Shuan put both hands round her glass and stared ahead of her as she talked.

She said: 'I see now that it was beastly of me. But when it began I was sort of fascinated with the idea. And when I did begin to find something out about Justin I made up my mind I *must* go on, because that would help Roger as well as—being a kind of revenge for his selling Deirdre. I *hated* him for that—'

'You could have appealed to Mr. Carnehill over Deirdre,' Joanna pointed out.

'But I told you—I wouldn't have done that for *anything*.'

'All right. Go on—'

'Well, it seemed easy, because Justin never bothered to make much secret of the fact that he was doing better out of something than he did out of his salary as agent for Roger, and that he could afford to pay Magda well too. I don't know why he wasn't afraid I should tell Roger what he had hinted at. But I didn't. I thought if I let him go on I should find out enough myself.'

'You could have told me!' put in René gently.

Shuan answered, 'I didn't want to bring you into it. I *wanted* to do it all myself. I began to go about with Justin because I hoped he would tell me more, especially when—when he was in one of those beastly boastful moods, when he didn't care much what he said—'

Joanna shivered involuntarily. How *could* Shuan have believed she could afford to play with fire to this extent?

The girl went on: 'He took me to Dublin with him. That was when I met Magda and the two men we were going to meet at

221

Musveen today. Magda was supposed to go with him, but I think they must have quarrelled or something last night, and Justin said she had refused flatly to go. He asked me instead. And I said I would.'

'But *why*, Shuan? You *must* have known that Justin was far more clever than you, and that he would never have given you enough to prove anything against him. It would always have been your word against his—against his *and* Magda's!'

Shuan's full red mouth set stubbornly. 'I hoped all along that he would do or say something which I could take straight to Roger as proof. It—It was only this afternoon that I suddenly saw how beastly *sordid* the whole thing was, and I began to hate myself for getting mixed up in it. We stopped for lunch at Ballyboy, and I was wondering then how I could get away and get back to Carrieghmere. But I hadn't any money, and I hadn't decided anything before I found myself getting back into the car again.

'And then I couldn't bear it any longer'—she put her hands over her face, so that they had difficulty in hearing her—'Justin began to boast again, and to talk as if we were in a sort of *partnership* together—it was horrible. Then I told him I wasn't going on—to Musveen or anywhere else. And I threatened that if he didn't stop the car I would jump. So he stopped it.

And—and then you came along!'

Gently René drew her hands down and held them closely between his.

'Haven't you wondered why we came, *chérie*? How we knew where you had gone? Do you realize that Magda told us? That she told us something else too?'

'Magda told you—?'

'Yes. She had already told the police of the rendezvous at Musveen. They would have been there waiting for you. *That* was why we had to follow you!'

'Oh—!' The girl's realization of what she had escaped was poignant to see. She said slowly: 'You let Justin go on?'

'I tried to warn him, but he wouldn't listen,' Joanna told her. 'There doesn't seem to be anything we can do about him until Mr. Carnehill knows all about it.'

Shuan shivered. 'Roger! He'll have to know! How he'll *despise* me!'

'He can't despise you. However mistakenly, you did what you did—for him,' said Joanna.

And René said: 'He can't despise you. For no one shall dare to despise the woman who I ask to be my wife!'

There was a moment of charged silence. Joanna's heart seemed to turn over in pity for René, who could court so boldly the reply which Shuan, loving Roger, must give him . . .

But Shuan's eyes were shining. Her hands were still clasped between his, and it was as if her surrender of them were eloquent of all else that she had to give him. For she said: 'You—you're asking me to *marry* you?'

'Yes, Shuan—'

'Oh, I will. I will! René darling, I *love* you so!'

Joanna stood up, a hand at her throat. She felt that she could almost hate Shuan for what she did—to René, who loved her and who did not understand...

René stood up too. The smile he gave Joanna came from the depth of his happiness as he said deprecatingly: 'It is almost unique—yes?—that a proposal of marriage is made before a third person! But you are so good a friend, Mademoiselle Joanna, that we do not care.'

'But *I* care!' Joanna's voice was taut and throbbing. 'Shuan, you can't—you *dare not*—marry René if it's Roger that you love!'

She knew that René's face had whitened as he looked quietly at Shuan and back at her. But Shuan said wonderingly: 'Roger? But I don't *love* Roger!'

René's tension relaxed, but Joanna's held. As if it were a stranger speaking, she heard herself say: 'Once—I asked you. And you said that you cared for Roger—terribly!'

It was Shuan's voice now which seemed to come from a long way off. Shuan said: 'So I do. I suppose I've loved Roger for almost as long as I can remember. But not as I love René—*not like that!*'

CHAPTER FOURTEEN

For a long time afterwards, whenever she re-lived that moment, Joanna could recall the whole incongruous scene. The unnatural sheen of the oilcloth upon the sloping table-top, the dusty grey-brown of the dry reed-heads, Shuan staring at her, and René muttering something about 'going to find Michael'—as if he sensed that there was something here in which he had no part.

Joanna said slowly as if expressing it for herself would help her to believe it: 'You mean—you've *never* loved Roger—as a woman does love a man?'

Shuan blushed a lovely colour. 'No, never like that. When I told you I cared terribly about him I didn't know you could possibly think *that!*'

'Are you sure'—it was an unworthy suspicion which spoke—'that you didn't *want* me to think it?'

But Shuan's frank stare was utterly disarming. 'No. Why should I?'

'I'm sorry, Shuan. Of course there wasn't any reason. But you were jealous of me,

225

weren't you? You were jealous of the things I could do for him and you could not. And I thought that perhaps you said what you did in order to—to establish your own rights—the right of your love for him.'

'Well, I was jealous,' admitted Shuan. 'You see, up till the time you came I'd been able to—to—' She paused, frowning. 'I can't think of the word which means that you try to do all you can to make up for something you have done earlier—something wicked or horrible, perhaps?'

Joanna was puzzled. 'I don't know. Compensate? Expiate?—that would be too strong—'

'No, it wouldn't. Expiate is what I wanted. I'd been able to expiate the horrible part I had played in his accident by doing absolutely everything I could for him—giving up my own time to him, trying never to grumble when he was beastly and bad-tempered, because all the time I had to be telling myself that it was my fault!'

'But I don't understand?' queried Joanna.

Shuan's eyes widened. 'Do you mean no one has told you? Didn't *Roger* tell you?'

'About his accident? I knew that you were out riding together when his horse shied and threw him.'

'You didn't know that it happened because I was playing the fool on my mare? That Roger had asked me to ride quietly because

226

his horse was tetchy and frisky, and that he was having difficulty in holding him in? I laughed and teased him about his being able to manage anything under a rein, and I *deliberately* tried to egg him on to join in some fancy stuff. His mount wouldn't stand for it, and almost the next thing I knew was that Roger was thrown, and that it was my fault! Do you mean Roger never told you?'

'No, he didn't tell me.' If Shuan's story were true, Joanna felt utterly humble before Roger's loyalty of silence.

'I thought you knew, and that you were *judging* me as I felt everyone—Mums and everybody—was doing. Sometimes I felt I hated people for it ... But it helped to set my teeth and to determine that, to make up for what I'd done, I'd give—and give—and give—to Roger until no one would *dare* to judge me, because I should have—expiated what I'd done in the first place. Then you came—'

'—And you began to feel hurt and unwanted and in the way,' asked Joanna gently.

'Yes. And then I began to feel that I must get away at any cost. That was when I talked to you ... I thought that *then* Roger might miss me, might want me back. I thought you knew all about the accident by then, and perhaps I did say that about caring for him because I wanted you to realize how much

227

you had usurped *my* place with him. But I didn't mean I *loved* him. I couldn't. He's always been like my brother—'

'Poor Shuan! You do live intensely, don't you?' Joanna's voice was tender and full of understanding.

'What do you mean?'

Joanna hesitated, wondering how to express, without hurting the girl's feelings, all that exaggeration of emotion, of self-dramatization which she seemed to bring to her every act. She said slowly: 'Well, you cared about the accident more than anyone need; and you tried to serve Roger perhaps even beyond your own powers. Then there was all this about Justin—am I right in thinking that you wouldn't even appeal to Roger about the sale of Deirdre the mare, because of some sort of guilt you still felt over the accident?'

Shuan nodded. 'Yes. I—do seem to make trouble for myself and—everyone, don't I?' Her lip quivered. 'Am I *like* that, Joanna? Shan't I ever be able to help it?'

'I don't know. But I think that people like you, who live so deeply and care so much, may bring as much happiness as they're likely to bring trouble to those they love. You've made René very happy, Shuan. Won't you tell me about that? How long have you known that you were in love with him?'

'I think I knew soon after we began to train

228

Lady of Belmont for the Show. Before that, I had been flattered by his wanting to be with me, to do things for me. Then when he began to help me with Lady of Belmont, we began to talk ... He told me about Belgium and I told him about when I was a little girl ... and he knew what I felt about Roger. And then, one morning, he kissed me—' Joanna, watching could see that Shuan was wrapped about in the radiance of that memory. 'And I told him not to be silly. And—he didn't do it again. It was after that that I knew I wanted him to—and that I wanted everything we were doing together then to go on all through our lives. I knew I couldn't bear it if it didn't. I dreaded the thought that he should stop wanting me. But when I began to go about with Justin he made no sign. So I had that to put up with too, as well as what all the rest of you were thinking about me! And it wasn't until today that I knew he had never stopped loving me, and that I had never stopped loving him!'

Shuan's voice sank to silence. Then, half shyly, she glanced at Joanna. 'That's what it was like for me. Joanna, when—when you go back to London, I hope it'll be like that for you too.'

'When I go back to London?'

'Yes. When you marry that man you're engaged to.'

'But I'm not engaged to anyone!'

'Well—sort of. I mean that man you went to see in Dublin—the one who came out to Carrieghmere.'

'But I'm not engaged to him. I never was. And I expect by this time he's married to somebody else—'

'Oh, Joanna, I'm sorry! I didn't know—truly I didn't. Do—do you mind terribly?'

A half smile played about Joanna's lips. 'No. You see, though we had always been good friends, it wasn't "like that" for us. It never had been, and we were fortunate enough to find out in time.'

'How did you find out?'

'I think it was by being away from each other for a while when I came over to Eire. Things seemed to fall into focus better ... and I began to be afraid that Dale and I were missing something. And when I saw him again it was like trying to blow upon dead ashes, hoping that just a single spark would glow for us. And when it didn't, the only thing to do was to admit that—the fire had never been alive at all.'

'You'd never been in love!' said Shuan with an air of clarifying the matter.

Joanna smiled. 'No. We'd never been in love,' she echoed.

Again Shuan said impulsively: 'Joanna, I'm sorry. You see, I was terribly jealous of you at first—you were so capable and cool and everything that I wasn't—and even when I began to like you and be grateful to you for Roger's sake, I didn't seem to be able to show it. But today I know that I want you to be happy—wherever happiness lies for you. Do you suppose,' she added ingenuously, 'that that's because, if they let me marry René, I know I'm going to be so happy that I want to share it?'

'I expect so. Happiness is like that—it has to bubble over. But don't worry about me, Shuan. I shall be happy. I've got my work. And my mother used to quote a Spanish proverb which said, "When one door shuts, another opens." When Dale and I parted we shut a door on something which had never existed. One day another door will open—for me.'

It was the same philosophy which she had expressed to Roseen that morning. She had guessed then that she had voiced it as much for herself as for the younger girl. In the days to come she would have to remind herself of it often. And it would help . . .

But Shuan was savouring it too. She repeated slowly: '"Another door opens—" Do you know, in a way that's what has happened to me? I mean, I made that sort of vow to myself that, because his accident was my fault, I'd sacrifice everything to Roger. And then you came, and I was hurt because I could see how much more value you were to

231

him than I was and how he was beginning to care for you—So that it was like another door opening for me when I suddenly found that none of it mattered so much after all, because I was falling in love with René—'

She stopped. Joanna said rather shakily: 'You use the words "care for" in strange places, Shuan!'

'But I don't! Not this time. I mean them. I *mean* that Roger was falling in love with you. I knew it. He knew it himself. It was when he learned about the man in London that he began to fight against it. You could see it happening. He didn't *want* to go on loving you when you belonged to somebody else. Roger is proud—and that's the way his pride works—'

Joanna stood up. 'That's not true, Shuan. You're letting your imagination run away with you. In any case, even if it were true, you would be betraying his confidence by telling me—'

'I would not! Roger has never talked to me about you. It's something that I just *know* about him. You probably think you have to snub me, because of professional etiquette or something. But I want Roger to be happy. Even when I was hideously jealous of you I'd have tried to be glad if he had asked you to marry him. I mightn't have succeeded very well then. But I'd be terribly glad now.' Suddenly the smudged greenish-blue eyes clouded with tears of sheer weariness, and Joanna put a protective arm about the girl's thin shoulders as she drew her towards the door.

'René and Michael will be waiting. Let's go home,' she said gently.

But Shuan held back. 'You haven't said whether, if he asked you now, you would say yes,' she accused childishly.

It was Joanna's turn to be conscious of a wave of utter weariness. 'Shuan, *please*! You don't understand. There are a dozen reasons against it!'

'But would any of them matter,' asked Shuan simply, 'if there were just one reason on the other side—*that you loved each other*?'

Joanna's glance dropped before the importunate innocence in the shadowed eyes raised to hers. She said, in a tone which was meant to be brisk with finality, but which was merely sharp with unspoken pain: 'Roger doesn't love me. He never has done. He's longing for me to leave Carrieghmere—'

'He told you that? But don't you see that was only his pride talking? That he must have made up his mind that he can do without you, if he must?'

'No. I've never been any more to him than a crutch he is able to discard. And it's Carrieghmere that matters to him now.'

'If he had been able to believe that you loved him he would have *shared* Carrieghmere

233

with you,' said Shuan slowly. 'Joanna, you've said that you don't think he loves you. But do you love *him*?'

It was the question Joanna had dreaded. And though she made no answer in words she was conscious that her very silence might have told Shuan too much.

* * *

In the car, when they were still miles from Carrieghmere, Shuan began to shiver uncontrollably. René wrapped a rug about her and tucked his own coat round her shoulders. But Joanna could tell from her racing pulse and flushed face that she was at the outset of a fever which would need more than mere blanketing. She urged Michael to drive at top speed again, knowing that time was all important in getting Shuan to bed and under Dr. Beltane's care.

Upon their arrival at Carrieghmere she was to realize that, as she had feared, their decision to leave no message for Roger had been unwise. For it seemed that, on his own arrival home, Roseen had been waiting for him with an excitable tale of woe of which he had been able to make little sense.

His greeting was uncompromising. 'Where have you been?' he demanded. 'What has Shuan been doing?'

'Roger—!' His name was no more than a

234

sigh of exhaustion upon Shuan's lips. By now the girl was near to collapse, and Joanna's protective arm about her shoulders tightened its clasp.

'Shuan isn't well,' she said briefly. 'I'm going to put her to bed and I'd like Dr. Beltane called at once, please.'

She turned away, drawing Shuan with her. She sensed that Roger had resented her authoritative tone. But after a moment's hesitation he said quietly: 'Very well, I'll see to it.'

Shuan began to cry softly, and Joanna, glancing at René, knew that he was longing to comfort her. She said gently: 'René, will you tell Mr. Carnehill all that we know ourselves—all that Shuan has told us?'

René nodded gratefully. 'Immediately! She—she will be—all right?' he added in a whisper.

'Very soon, I hope. But she's very, very tired!'

She took Shuan up to bed then and as, with the unhurried skill which was second nature to her cool hands, she performed the deft tasks which made all the difference to the girl's comfort, she told herself that in her work alone would she find, one day, the serene contentment which would overlay pain. For while you worked you had no urge to think ... to question ... to remember. And day-long, healthy tiredness might even banish dreams...

She stayed with Shuan until Dr. Beltane came. When he had examined her and they had left her room together, he commented: 'Well, she's in the sort of nervous condition that would give the "come hither" to any wandering germ. She lives at a great rate, to be sure. What do you suppose she has been up to lately to get herself into that state?'

'She's been worrying needlessly. But principally, I think, she's been falling in love!'

The doctor's astonishment was gratifying. 'Falling in love, eh? Bless my soul, what's the new generation coming to? When I was young we took that sort of thing in our stride—we didn't run temperatures over it! And where in the bog would she have found anyone to fall in love *with*, when she'd not take a second glance at the Belgian fellow spreading himself to make a mat for her feet?'

'It *is* René Menden,' smiled Joanna.

'You mean she's taken him? And to think I was sorely tempted to tell him his technique was all wrong—that the girls don't want 'em faithful—they'd rather have 'em masterful any day! Looks as if I was wrong—I'm glad I didn't interfere. But tell me, is she being crossed in love? Is the family proving difficult?'

'I don't think anyone knows, so far. It was only today that they admitted to each other

236

that they both wanted the same thing.'

'And where's the young man now?'

'He's with Mr. Carnehill. Mrs. Carnehill should be back from Dublin soon—Michael will have gone to meet her train—'

She broke off as at that moment Mrs. Carnehill came hurrying upstairs looking puzzled and worried. At sight of them she exclaimed:

'Joanna, what's happened? Michael was late meeting me, because he said he'd had to be driving you and René more than half-way to the border—that you were following Shuan somewhere! He said you had brought her back—"and she, unable to stand on her feet at the latter end"—that's how he put it—and he had some version of his own that she had been trying to run away with *Justin*, though, of course, I knew that couldn't be true—'

The fear that Michael's story might indeed prove to have some truth in it spoke in her face, and Dr. Beltane put a reassuring arm round her shoulders. 'And for what,' he demanded, 'would she be running away with a man like McKiley? Rest easy now, Edna Carnehill! All that's wrong with Shuan is that she has a little fever that she won't be long getting over, though Nurse here tells me she's also got a little fever of another kind that she won't *want* to be getting over!'

He chuckled flatly at his own joke, but Mrs. Carnehill's bright face creased into

237

greater bewilderment than before. 'Robert Beltane, don't be exasperating! What has Shuan been *doing*?'

Joanna put a hand upon her arm. 'René has asked Shuan to marry him, and I was there when she said Yes,' she said quietly. 'René is with Mr. Carnehill now, explaining everything, but Shuan was taken ill suddenly and I brought her straight to bed.'

'Shuan? *René*? But what's all this about Justin? Oh, dear, let me go to the child—!'

In the hall below, the telephone shrilled, interrupting her. The door of Mrs. Carnehill's study opened and Roger went to lift the receiver. As he did so he glanced up, saw his mother, and beckoned to her to go down to him. She did so, followed by Joanna and Dr. Beltane. They stood, a silent little knot, intuitively guessing that the message Roger took had significance for them all.

His own part in it consisted almost wholly of monosyllables.

'Yes ... Yes ... Where? I see. Tomorrow morning? ... Yes, of course ... No, I think not ... Thank you.'

He laid down the receiver, stood for a moment without speaking, then turned to face them.

'McKiley has been arrested at Musveen on the border. Two other men charged with smuggling drugs were arrested with him, and the police have a warrant for searching the

238

Dower House for evidence tomorrow.'

Mrs. Carnehill gasped, and her voice was no more than a whisper as she asked: 'Shuan? Roger—*Shuan isn't involved?*'

He opened his arms to her, and she went to them trustingly. 'Poor Mother!' he said gently. 'You are completely in the dark, aren't you? No, Shuan isn't involved. There's nothing wrong with Shuan—' He paused. He had been looking down at his mother's bent head, but now he looked straight across and into Joanna's eyes. 'Except,' he said slowly, 'that perhaps she has loved—too much.'

CHAPTER FIFTEEN

Shuan tossed restlessly all night and Joanna spent most of it at her bedside. When Dr. Beltane came he said that she might be feverish for some days, but added dryly: 'She has her best medicine handy—down at the Dower House! You may let the boy see her whenever you think fit, Nurse.'

'But—'

He looked quickly at Joanna. 'Oh, I forgot. When were you leaving?'

'On Thursday.'

'Well, Mrs. Carnehill will need help with Shuan for a week or two. If I wired your matron you'd have no objection to staying on, would you?'

'No, Doctor, none.'

'Then that's settled. Everyone here would rather have you about than somebody new.' Dr. Beltane trotted towards the door, but as he reached it. 'By the way, I didn't get near enough to you at Shuan's dance to congratulate you on your Clarissa Carnehill get-up. It was a grand-idea.' The shrewd eyes beneath the bushy brows held hers. 'Forgive me for an old busybody,' said Dr. Beltane. But as he turned to go he added cryptically: 'Do you know, on my way out I'm going to have another look at Clarissa. I've always thought that quiet smile of hers was very wise. I wonder what she was wise about?'

*   *   *

By late afternoon Shuan seemed better, so Joanna allowed her to sit up in bed and to see René, who had come on shy tiptoe to her door.

Warning him not to let Shuan talk too much, she left them together and went downstairs, where she found Mrs. Carnehill alone.

'How is Shuan now?' asked the older woman anxiously.

'Much better and very happy, I think,' smiled Joanna. 'René is with her, and I left them holding hands across the coverlet and not uttering a word!'

'Bless them! You know, Joanna, it's odd and rather sad, the way the nursery folk can steal a march like that! Of course it was never possible to miss what René felt about *her*. But Shuan has always seemed such a child! To think of her twisting about in her head all that fantastic idea of her responsibility to Roger, and that dangerous dabbling in Justin's affairs—And now, wanting to marry René—it takes my breath away! And René, of course, wants to marry Shuan at once!'

'You mean he'll take her back to Belgium with him?'

'Well, I don't think René has worked that out yet. But Roger and I sat up late last night, talking. And he said then that he would like to keep René on here to help him with the estate when this wretched business about Justin is all cleared up. If René agreed, Roger's idea was that they should have the Dower House.'

'But—'

'I know what's in your mind! You were going to say that when Roger marries the Dower House should be my home. But, as I said to Roger, the place will be big enough for three when the time comes—even if they have to give me a kitchen of my own to experiment in!'

'René and Shuan should be very happy there,' said Joanna thoughtfully.

'Yes. I hope René will stay, though Roger hasn't been able to talk to them yet. He's been busy all day with the police—questions, questions, questions! But I saw them drive away, I think, so I'm expecting him back from the Dower House very soon now. Could he go and talk to Shuan while René is there?'

'Yes, of course.'

'I'll tell him, then. But you're looking pale, Joanna. Why don't you go out and get some air?'

Glad of the opportunity, Joanna turned towards the door. When she came back she learned that Roger had already gone up to see Shuan, and she herself did not go to the girl's room until it was time for her to be settled in for the night.

Joanna noticed that she was still flushed, but the fact that her temperature and pulse were almost normal showed that it was a glow of happiness and no longer of fever. She accepted Joanna's attentions in a kind of rapt silence, doing as she was told with dreamy automatic obedience.

But when she was really tucked between the cool sheets and Joanna was ready to leave she asked suddenly: 'Have you heard about us—that I can marry René and still not have to go away from Carrieghmere?'

'Yes. I'm so glad,' Joanna assured her warmly.

Shuan turned shining eyes upon her.

'That's what's so marvellous about you—you really are glad. And I was such a beastly jealous pig about you! You know'—her brow wrinkled in perplexity—'I've got to be grateful to so many people at once! To you for being so patient with me all along. And to René—oh, for *everything*! And to both of you for being just in time to take me away from Justin—And to Roger, for letting René stay! Joanna, what can I *do* to pay you all back?'

Joanna smiled down at the anxious face upon the pillow. 'Do nothing, Shuan. You can't run your life on a sort of balancing account of "payings-back" or rewards or expiations.' She saw Shuan wince at the memory the last word evoked and she hurried on: 'You see, none of us have done anything for you but because we may have loved you or understood you or wanted you to be happy. In the same circumstances you might have done the same for any of us. But you can't *deliberately* weigh gratitude against gratitude or love against love—'

Shuan turned her face into the pillow, so that her dark hair spread fanwise upon the sheets. Joanna bent over in order to sweep it gently back, and it was only in doing so that she was able to catch Shuan's whispered words.

'But I've done *something*! I *had* to! I sent René away and then I told Roger—'

'*Shuan!* What did you tell him?'

'That—that you'd never really loved the man in London. I told him you had said so ... And I told him I had asked you about loving *him*—Roger himself, I mean—but that you hadn't answered, and I hadn't dared to ask you again.'

It was in utter dismay that Joanna protested. 'Shuan dear, you may have meant so well—but you betrayed my confidence by telling Roger anything about Dale Woodward and—and me!'

'I can't care—I couldn't have let you go away without his knowing. You mustn't be angry with me.' Her voice was tremulous, and Joanna recognized that in her present state she could not take a scolding or even criticism. Shuan went on with a gulp: 'Roger didn't say anything for a while, and when he did he didn't even mention you. Do you know what he said? He asked me if I believed I really loved René, and whether, if there were anything to stop my marrying him, except perhaps that he belonged to someone else and didn't want me at all, I'd accept the way things were for an instant. And when I said, No, of course not, but hadn't he heard what I told him about you, he laughed and kissed me, and said, "Bless you, Shuan darling. 'Out of the mouths of babes and sucklings.—'" And then he went away!'

*   *   *

244

The dawn of the August morning which already held the promise of autumn found Joanna waking from the first sleep which had come to her since she had gone to her room after leaving Shuan, sending a message to Mrs. Carnehill by Roseen that she was tired and was going straight to bed. All night she had been upon the alert lest Shuan should need her. That was her trained body ready to spring to duty. But her mind had been awake in a different way. Back and forth ran her thoughts . . . Shuan had even told him of that question which she had been unable to answer . . . And he had made no sign that Shuan's cruel betrayal had any significance for him whatever!

Last night she hadn't been able to bear to meet him. Yet today, and through all the subsequent days of her enchainment to Shuan and to her duty, she was going to have to meet him and address him casually, and see in his eyes the indifference that would be worse to face even than the cold scorn with which he had accused her of disloyalty on the night of Shuan's dance. From that, England and new work would be a refuge. But between her and England there lay what seemed a desert of shame . . .

For an hour she tried to sleep again. But sleep would not come. So she rose and dressed, twisted her hair into a looser knot than she would wear with her uniform and, noticing that it had been raining during the night, donned thick shoes and a raincoat. She would go out and walk ... and walk away thoughts and memories and desires...

Out of doors the atmosphere was fresh. She took her favourite path across the park; at a far gate it led out on to the flat ribbon of road which bordered the estate, and on the other side of which lay what Roger had once called 'the interminable bog'.

But she had come to love the bog ... its colours, the uncharted stretches of it between the well-trodden ways which carried no hazards for the unwary, and the indescribable scent of the turf which in absence would be a nostalgia for the heart. She was glad that Shuan's thoughts would not have to ache in homesickness for it. But her own—?

She had been walking for only about ten minutes when she believed she heard footsteps behind her. But the bog mist had begun to wreathe patchily and she could see nothing. The steps came on; the mist lifted, and she turned to see Roger striding towards her, intent, purposeful and not to be avoided unless she took deliberately to the bog.

He came on. Since she knew that he realized she had seen him she could not turn away. As he overtook her she glanced at him quickly and believed that she saw in his face the indifference which she had felt sure would be there.

He said: 'You're out early!'

'Yes. I'd been on the watch for Shuan all night and I couldn't sleep.'

'Neither could I. And as this is my day for taking Tom o' the Moor two ounces of tobacco I thought he might as well have it.'

'Tom o' the Moor? Oh, yes, the old man who lives over there and cuts turf for a living.'

Roger nodded. 'Yes—when he isn't engaged on less legitimate forms of livelihood, the old spalpeen—! Would you go along with me? Have you time?'

For answer Joanna turned to walk at his side. Her heart was pounding, but she was relieved at the ease with which casual, impersonal talk came. She sought anxiously for something else to say about old Tom. She began: 'You mean he—?' But mistakenly she looked up into Roger's unguarded face, and her own eyes dropped before what she saw there.

'Joanna!' It was a cry more than it was a spoken name. 'I didn't come out to go over to Tom o' the Moor's! I came because I watched you come out, and I had to find you, because I was afraid you would go on trying to avoid me as you did last night when Shuan must have told you all that she had told me! Joanna, I've been a fool, a proud fool, an over-scrupulous fool who wouldn't try to win

247

something he believed belonged—had ever belonged—to another man! From the first day I've loved you and been afraid of you and fought against you—and not known what I'd do with my life when you had gone. I *love* you, Joanna. Does it say anything to you at all?'

Gently he took her wrists and drew her hands from the pockets of the raincoat where they had been clenched, nails thrusting into palms. They lay upwards in his, the mute surrender of all she had to give. She answered him softly. 'It says all I wanted to hear—all I shall ever want!'

They stood there holding hands, as if afraid by a closer contact to break the magic of a spell which lay around them.

Joanna said: 'I've loved you too. It was something which I couldn't tell Shuan in so many words, for I had to tell you—and if not you, then never. But you love Carrieghmere. And at Carrieghmere I'm no more than alien, a stranger—'

'A stranger? You? When you've come to be the very core of my life that's belonged to Carrieghmere ever since I was born, and back through all the people behind me? Farther back even than Clarissa, Joanna! That night—when I looked at you for the first time—didn't my eyes tell you *anything* of all I wanted to say?'

'I thought you would hate me for it—!'

'I hated what I saw as the—the *damnable* likeness that could make you seem so much part of us, of all we have and are—and yet keep you separate and aloof and not-belonging of your own will, because you had other ties, other loves—'

'And yet you wanted me to go. You said so! You wanted to possess Carrieghmere again, to be free of me, of all I stood for in your mind—your helplessness and your dependence on the things I could give!'

'Dear Joanna! Don't you realize that that day when I told you you must go, I was throwing myself upon your pity for the first time—hoping and praying that you would realize my utter, *utter* need of you? When you snubbed me—you said something brutal about sentimentality or over-emotionalism—I got proud again. I'd asked, and you hadn't answered. And nothing would make me ask again. At the dance I was still angry, and I believed too that you might actually have encouraged Shuan's friendship with McKiley. Then when you went with René to bring Shuan back—to try to save her and all of us from scandal—I believed that you must care a little for us—that the thing that's Carrieghmere might mean something to you, even if I never could. That's all, Joanna. So much of all this might have been said before, but perhaps it would have meant less. *Now* there's nothing but—sureness—in front!'

She went to him then and his arms closed about her. He said: 'Mother knew. We talked for a long time last night. She made you play Clarissa because she thought it might *force* me to see ... But long before that she wanted you for a daughter—as I want you, need you, *desire* you—for a wife!'

Their lips met in a promise which gave all, hoped all, understood all. The future might lie as uncharted as the reedy bog around them. But their blood would spring to the challenge of it in the eternally sweet cycle of mating, of which they both had been made.

Photoset, printed and bound in Great Britain by REDWOOD PRESS LIMITED, Melksham, Wiltshire